White Elephants

S T O R I E S

White Elephants

S T O R I E S

Angelo R. Lacuesta

Anvil

MANILA

White Elephants: Stories
by Angelo R. Lacuesta

Copyright by ANGELO R. LACUESTA, 2005

Published and exclusively distributed by
ANVIL PUBLISHING INC.
8007-B Pioneer St., Bgy. Kapitolyo,
Pasig City 1603 Philippines
Sales & Marketing: 637-3621; 637-5141;
        747-1622; 747-1624; anvilpublishing@yahoo.com
Fax: 637-6084

The National Library of the Philippines CIP Data

Recommended entry:

Lacuesta, Angelo R.
    White elephants: stories / Angelo R. Lacuesta.
–Pasig City : Anvil Pub., 2005
    1 v

    1. Short stories, Philippine (English).
I. Title.

PL5546 899.21'03 2005 P051000164
ISBN 971-27-1588-4 (bp)
ISBN 971-27-1679-1 (np)

Cover design by ANGELO R. LACUESTA
Interior design by ANI V. HABÚLAN

Printed in the Philippines

The author wishes to thank the following:

Chin, Georgia and Ashley Martelino for the elephant. Gregorio C. Brillantes for his guidance and generosity. Mikey and Lou Samson for the anecdotes. Kim Silos, Copagi Joson, Chuck Ramos and Noel Perez. Jose Y. Dalisay and Alfred A. Yuson for their support. Mabi David for important advice. Mike Manalo at Logika. Karina Bolasco and Ani Habúlan at Anvil. The Hawthornden International Retreat for Writers for time and space. Lolita Rodriguez-Lacuesta, Kite, Gabby and Andi for the usual.

Earlier versions of "White elephants," "Procession," "Leather" and "Rest stop" appeared in the *Philippines Free Press*. An earlier version of "Self with dog, 1997" appeared in *Philippine Graphic*. "Thousand year eve" was published online in *The Best Philippine Short Stories*. "Nilda" appeared, in a different form, in *Future Shock: Prose*, an edition of *Sands and Coral*.

Contents

White elephants   1

Procession   19

Thousand year eve   33

Rest stop   46

New wave days   55

Nilda   68

Self with dog, 1997   80

Ghosts   92

Leather   112

"Untitled"   121

Glossary   129

White elephants

MONICA WAS A SINGLE MOTHER. THE ACCIDENT HAPPENED WHILE she was living in with her boyfriend. For all their years of argument and betrayal, it took a single reconciliatory night for her daughter to be conceived.

"But I knew," she always tells me, "I knew I was pregnant right then and there." I don't know what to do with that kind of self-knowledge, that kind of woman's wisdom. I look at her, and this wisdom challenges mine. Like the child was an accident and not an accident. It's a story she has told me many times, and the repeated telling has left it stony and isolated inside my stomach.

Soon after the child was born, she continues, she could not take it anymore and walked out of his life carrying the baby in her arms. That actually took the span of long and difficult months.

I introduce her to me, to her, to us, to the mirror that hangs faithfully and treacherously over the bed, revealing bodies growing fat and old and tired. I'd like you to meet my wife. She's thirty years old, five-foot-five, with black hair and black eyes. She's had one child, suffered a couple of

1

miscarriages but she still has a lot of years in her. And our long and difficult months will soon be over. I say this with certainty because either we will walk out of this dirty motel separated, or we will end up working it out again. I say it also because I, too, have her woman's wisdom. After all, I am a man of thirty-one who has been married to this woman three years now. And, to add to that: her child, Juliana, now unofficially our child, waits for us in Manila while we wait out the rain in a godforsaken motel whose name I have even forgotten, at the edge of a city far from my own.

The American Naval Base occupied seventy thousand hectares of flat and rolling land, strategically cradled in the null space between low mountains, dark and heavy rainforests and a wide bay. The air here, even by the sea, is hot and stifling, hemmed in by the rainforest and clouded up with stirred-up dust. But today, all the dust has been beaten down by a freakish accident of hard rain and wind.

The super typhoon—as the announcer on the radio has called it—has threatened to rip up the roofs and lawns of the white and green houses on the base. They are American-style bungalows and two-storey houses, sitting back on subdivided plots of bluegrass, with windowpanes like eyeglasses and steel screen doors like rigid mouths. There are other curious sights: mailboxes on poles, white picket fences and garages large enough to hold Buicks, Tauruses and Cadillacs. Only the tropical heat and the surrounding rainforest subtract from the impression this city gives of America.

The roads are winding and well paved, laid out on the zone like a lattice of bamboo scaffolding. Closer to the bay, the grid straightens itself out, to accommodate the M-1 Abrams tanks and armored personnel carriers that rolled along the paved grid connecting the servicemen's cottages, the

2

barracks and the tactical command centers. Battleships, cruisers and the occasional aircraft carrier once sat in the bay, watching, waiting, radar and sonar spinning. And along the airstrips on the edge of the base, camouflaged by the hedge of rainforest, nested the dark, radar-proof Blackbirds and swept-wing Tomcats.

Occasionally there would be a rush, a take-off, perhaps marked only by a white cloud on the tarmac. When the Blackbird flew, it must have banked lazily around the base, its blackness unmarred except for two white American stars. Then it would jump forward as though time suddenly straightened itself out, leaving a sonic boom that was heard for miles around, reverberating through the rainforest and the mountain passes.

The next sonic clap that was heard was the sound of the mountain itself, unleashing yet another accident. It sent American GIs into helicopters and C-130s, never to return. The pyroclastic flow, a rain of mud and ash, prompted an emergency evac and turned Subic City into empty wasteland.

The process of rebuilding and scavenging began shortly, driven by political and economic eruptions. Abandoned cars, truck and equipment were auctioned off. The base became a special economic zone, harboring processing plants, semiconductor factories and duty-free price clubs. They drove in by the busload from Manila, hungry for crates of cheap corned beef, half-priced running shoes, stacks of corn chips and cheese balls. But with the years that followed came more political issues and economic measures, bringing another change, another wind. Subic City ceased being a city, not even a real town, and the wide roads, the green plains, white buildings and low houses now make for nothing but a weekend resort scavenged from bunkers, warehouses and housing for

3

American GIs, all repackaged into breathing space for city dwellers like us.

We live in a cramped old house on Polaris St., just off Makati Avenue, hemmed in by KTV bars and Korean restaurants. My mother-in-law's family built it when she was very young. At the time, there was no Makati Business District yet, just a cluster of low buildings on a short strip of road. There was nothing in our area but tall grass and dirt road. When my mother-in-law died we appropriated the upper floor and left the ground floor empty and unfurnished. We didn't make much money, and we thought we'd wait for tenants or borders. Once we had the happy idea of converting the area into a small café. "For hungry architects," I offered.

Upstairs, our living space consists of an area large enough for a drafting table, a white couch, two wicker chairs and a TV set. This connects to a master bedroom, a smaller room for Juliana, and a shared bathroom. I had the walls repainted and the solid wood floor repaired and polished. I had the eaves fixed, the roof retiled, the spaces between the walls and below the roof fumigated. But I changed nothing else in the house.

I had the walls repainted and the solid wood floor repaired and polished. I had the eaves fixed, the roof retiled, the spaces between the walls and below the roof fumigated and treated. But I changed nothing else in the house.

The house has been designed so that during most hours of the daytime the living room is bathed in good air and a gentle, eggshell-colored light, filtered and recycled through brown wooden windows set with squares of white glass. I did nothing to the original plan. Our walls remain white and unencumbered by heavy molding and the foot-wide narra planks remain on our floor. It's a good house, small, solid,

4

square, simple. They don't build houses like this anymore. Now even the small mass housing units I once penciled by the dozen are made to look like Italian villas and mausoleums or Mediterranean dwellings with redundant balconies and tile roofs with unusable, impractical tile overhangs.

I CAME UPON MONICA AFTER THE BIG EARTHQUAKE IN 1990. WE FELT it all the way in Manila but it was Baguio that was the worst hit. In the mountain city the ground cracked open on the main streets, under cars, houses and people. People fell into the sudden chasms, or were crushed under layers of buildings. Six or seven hotels knelt broken and swaybacked on the ground. Aftershocks had made sure the roads that fed into the city were twisted beyond use or rendered impassable by boulders. The city was cut off, left suspended high in the empty air by the main earthquake. They choppered in TV crews in to investigate the damage. They needed warmth, food, clean water. Burnham Park had turned into a makeshift gathering of tents and the Baguio cathedral had become a refugee center.

Important people were stranded and hurt. A senator's wife lay trapped under the remains of a small hotel, its broken floors piled on top of each other. While waiting for the rescue teams she gave interviews through a small breathing hole. Others were not so lucky, she said, from the darkness of the hole. There were two or three people around her who had been crushed by falling pillars. After two days the hole began to stink of decaying flesh.

Investigations arose concerning the architectural soundness of the felled hotels. Some citizens filed criminal cases against the developers, the engineers and the architects. I shuddered at this, and thought of the designs I had done.

A television station set up relief centers in Manila, where they collected donations of food, canned goods and used clothing. They got volunteers to pack the relief goods into boxes before airlifting them out to the rest of Luzon. Monica and I were on the same assembly line packing pineapple chunks, instant noodles and tetra briks of juice.

Monica worked quietly, and hardly a word passed her lips as she counted the boxes of juice into cubic clusters of four. Years later Monica told me that she knew that I had been trying to catch her eye that afternoon. I had contrived to be assigned to the station beside her. After the volunteers' dinner I stepped out for a smoke. When I returned she had disappeared on me, just like that, leaving her relief boxes open and incomplete.

After that, I went back to my work, where I discovered the earthquake holiday had left me cracked and open. I could take no more of developers who wanted whole hectares of rolling land made to look like New England, or Southern France, or the Italian countryside. By the time I resigned I had designed a statue of St. Ignatius, a fountain for a beach resort that dwarfed Trevi, a subdivision clubhouse that was a variation on the temple on Mount Parnassus, and a cluster of stunted residential buildings that was my take on the Versailles. Architects are tempted to create monuments. Instead of marble or stone we poured concrete and painted it white. Corners were cut. Lines were fudged and history written, designed and built out of nothing, across centuries and oceans made of pure imagination, unfounded and unformed.

It was this culture that I imagined I was working hard to protect when I saw Monica again a year later, this time at an anti-US bases rally in front of the old Congress building. The senate was in a voting session on the US bases. The Americans had wanted to extend their lease on their military bases for another ten years. Later on the newspapers said there had been about a hundred fifty thousand of us in the crowd, not counting balut and cigarette vendors and the National Police. Monica wore a white shirt, faded jeans and sandals. When I saw her I instantly remembered her. It was raining hard, and I could see her standing quietly and perfectly still, on a concrete island with her arms crossed over her breasts. Through the sheets of rain the building appeared like an image from the past, as though it had just been built.

When the vote came through to end the Americans' tenure, the news swept through the crowd like radio waves rippling through the air. There were shouts of relief and they sang a song. People were hugging each other and crying. Through all the hysterics I saw Monica standing quietly. I walked up to her and saw that she recognized me and was happy to see a face she knew. I embraced her, and to my surprise she returned my warmth and passion.

The very first time I undressed her, I discovered stretch marks across her stomach and uncovered a scar, raised, hard, but very fine, hidden under the mesh of her pubic hair like a buried wire. I was puzzled then—and then, in the silence of my ministrations I suddenly understood. But she was still so beautiful, still very young, and I thought of myself as a still-young man who would do what it took to love. And that first time, it was so easy to love her, with the courage and perseverance that were strong enough to shape buildings and move governments.

An arm, a leg, an ear, a body. Made to walk, grasp, catch sound waves that fall off mouths and the atmosphere. Made

7

to open and receive my thrusts, my words, my notions. Soon after I recognized the telltale marks of childbirth I saw Monica as more than the sum of these. She was designed from without, not from within, shaped by her lover, her love child, by all the connections she once had, before suspending herself from them like a city trying to rip itself from its foundations.

She was shaped also by her mother, who lived with her in that beautiful small house. While she studied and went to demonstrations and did volunteer work, her mother took care of her child. In this way, Monica grew up building a life out her mother's life, and on that life she built hers, and on her mother's death we decided to build our house, for a new family that was Monica, her child and me.

It is easy to imagine what kind of sorrows and frustrations happened next. This sort of thing happens more than it doesn't. Someone told me that marriages are accidents waiting to happen: lock a man and a woman in a room, throw out the key, and watch and wait. At that time I was already working for a new firm, designing steel and glass office towers. On the side I had concerned myself with preserving the old Jai Alai building along Taft Avenue, one of Manila's busiest, craziest streets, choked up with jeepney traffic and coursing like a clogged vein under the shadow of the Light Rail Transit. The old Jai Alai building sat in the middle of the din, with a hemi-cylindrical glass façade and striped by a sculptured frieze that depicted the old Basque sport in its many attitudes. The city government saw the old Jai Alai building as either an eyesore or a symbol of the country's decadent colonial past. Here was a structure that was an arena for a Spanish game that had turned into an ugly vice. "The Sky Room," as it was named, in elegant Art Deco letters across its glassy face, was the venue for cocktails and evening parties during its heyday. Manila's elite would glance down from time to time at the

Spanish pelotaris hurling and bouncing balls. Still, it was an important architectural and cultural artifact.

At that time the Americans saw Manila as an important extension of their global plans. They brought in military leaders, prospectors and dealmakers, pioneers who could build businesses and establish markets. Then they brought in surveyors and city planners to lay down a grid of roads, bridges and businesses that they thought would connect, like a puzzle, with their own cities, cities like Chicago and San Francisco and New York.

It was about that time, too, that our house was built. My mother-in-law was only ten or twelve years old. She loved radio and television and American chocolates. She grew up listening to the Beatles and Elvis. Manila was an American city, filled with new ways to live and work, spreading and rising with ideas and happenings. She wore her hair long and her skirt very short. She had many lovers, and soon had a happening herself, this child she carried and delivered, and named after what was man's greatest achievement, the Apollo moon landing: Monica.

To all this built-up memory, the government's countermove was to tear the entire Jai Alai building down and in its place, erect a new Hall of Justice. Not only was it deemed practical and symbolic, but it also created jobs and lent an air of newness and vibrancy to the congested district.

There are other structures, beautifully complete, but in the memory of the city, completely forgotten. Buildings whose shells have long outlived their use. The old Metropolitan Theatre was another structure built in the Art Deco style, and has since been revived and left for dead a number of times. Now there is no more use for it, or the lot it stood on, so it has become a haunt of vagrants and glue-sniffers. Inside, the cushioned seats, the stage and the parterre boxes are kept in darkness.

Soon the room we had locked ourselves in had grown dark and different from the early days of our marriage. There were two of us in the shrinking room, plus a child in the adjoining quarters, and all the eggshell-white light did was let us see ourselves in starkness. I began to see Monica as half-formed and incomplete—a married woman that needed to bear the responsibility of a child before she could be whole.

In the mirror her body appears in full and clear detail, a phenomenon complete unto itself, oblivious to me, the powerless observer.

I've loved all kinds of women. I have been through so many of them, lived inside so many of them, that it has often become hard to distinguish the real me from them: their thoughts, their words, their gestures so simply and easily became mine. It's been said that when couples grow used to each other they start to look alike. I like to think it's because people start wearing their faces the same—pulling that same tired smile, or that same pained look, or that same fixed, blank expression. I have worn all of these faces, on and off, for most of my life, not just trying them on like masks or items of clothing. But building them, tearing them down, and rebuilding them like heavy edifices that are built up and torn down through seasons.

There are affairs that, in the thick of them, make us wish we weren't there. Our weekend habit is walking the malls. My habit, of late, when I am walking with her, is wondering whether I could simply disappear into the crowd that passes us by. I pick the right time, the right crowd, and by slipping into that unformed mass of teenagers, matrons and maids on their day off, I would lose her and she would lose me. But my hand grips hers tightly. When I was a child I got lost in the shopping arcades and department stores so many times that my parents had soon learned to play it cool—like me, who had gotten so used to it that getting lost was a natural process of life. A little like falling in love, perhaps. You get used to the swell, the anger and the loss. After that, you begin to accept everything as a sort of accident that's already happened.

The last time she walked out on me, we were in a taxicab waiting for the lights to change. There were no harsh words, no argument, no single thing you could talk about afterwards and blame like a piece of poor engineering. It was a long and careful build up, ending in one of those heavy silences when you look out your side of the cab. She simply opened the door and hit the sidewalk running. She didn't even slam the door but left it open. It was an incomplete move, one that I could take as an open invitation. But I had made a promise to myself about all that, and that after strike three that would be it. Still, she was one of those girls who made you feel like everything was strike two, that made you say to yourself the next time would be the last time, although it would actually be strike three, or thirteen, or thirty.

But I didn't move that day. I simply reached over and pulled the taxi door shut. I made a few excuses to the driver, and pretended to busy myself with a *Time* magazine. It felt to me like a silent victory, an occasion marked by nothing more than a quiet contentment and a trace of a smile. I was quite sure, too, that the driver had seen my expression. But we drove on.

In this city, in this country, buildings, hotels, condominium towers, convention centers are built, all with the regularity of a harvest. During this season, men and women celebrate with a feast that brings over townsfolk from neighboring villages.

11

Even the poorest house becomes an open house, the best plates and glasses are brought out, and the most secret family recipes are prepared. In the city, we have a rhythm too, much like this. During such swells, the markets go up and people rejoice: building and buying season once again. With the turning of the months, the land goes dry, the rains fail to fall, and the crops fail to flower. The politics changes and the banks bleed dry, corporations go under and deals turn sour, turning celebrated buildings into white elephants, half-formed shells, or empty lots.

On the way to the Jai Alai site I passed a six-storey shell of concrete and open air, with clusters of uncut, six-inch-diameter steel bars protruding seven or eight feet from its smooth cement face. Why, even on Makati Avenue, in the very nerve center of the business district, there rises a monolithic nothing made of grey, unpolished concrete, built by banks, subsidized by the government and now peopled only by ghosts and city birds, its upper floors still wrapped in heavy green netting, its temporary nature gaining permanence.

The taxi driver drove onward, through the city streets with surprising ease and speed until we hit solid traffic at the foot of the Nagtahan Bridge, forced by bridgeworks into a single lane. Some meters ahead where the bottleneck was at its thickest, there was a continuous stream of diesel smoke from a dump truck and the urgent sound of a jackhammer. In the smoke and the sound, the city looked and felt like there was an earthquake and it was going up in flames. The river itself was dark and moved slow, as though it were thickened with ash and upturned mud. It seemed like an emergency, like the whole city was being evacuated. I felt an urge to pay the driver, get off and pick my way through the bumpers and the tailpipes, until I reached the other side of the road where cars sped by. Foolish to return to a city that was slowly being

12

ravaged by fire and moving earth, I would hail a cab, hitch a ride, or snag a jeepney rail with an outstretched arm, and look for Monica, beginning at the exact spot where she stepped out of the taxi, and going out in concentric circles until I reached the end of the city. When I found her, of course, she would be half-alive, trampled underfoot, or worse, would still refuse to take my hand, even in the middle of a burning city.

There must be other worlds, other women. I ride the thought to its natural conclusion, like one of those new MRT trains you get on but can't escape because every exit is packed. I imagine the crowd slowly thinning as the train plods from stop to stop, until I am the only one in the train and the door beeps open and I emerge into another city, far from the woman I knew. It would be a dream city. My dream city, where everything works and there is no fear of getting lost or getting mugged, even while you are walking in the middle of the street, in the middle of the night. There would be museums, well-kept buildings, true monuments. A city with a vast network of asphalt roads and silent trains and quiet sidewalks, like Singapore, Frankfurt, or Paris.

13

Cities like Subic City, which is called a city but only almost is, with the white houses and buildings, the traffic lights, the vast hangars filled with US goods, its empty tarmacs littered with the spent fuselages of jet planes and trucks, its organized web of roads and right angled intersections, all abandoned once, abandoned twice, hermetically sealed at the borders and connecting nowhere and with no one.

We had a half-baked plan to rent one of those abandoned, refurbished, fully-furnished cottages and sit out the heat and find time for our own kind of r&r: release and reconciliation. I begin to think that coming here has been a bad idea to begin with. But Monica's manner tells me that it is a good idea to be dislocated sometimes, and to think and to plan.

But this rain is unplanned, blowing across the tar in hard sheets, so that even the road seems soft and powerless. Cars and buses switch on headlights and hazard blinkers. Yellow lines are blurred and washed away in the water. The rain has hemmed us in and driven us out, out of the old base and into surrounding Olongapo City. Our leisurely drive has been turned into a frantic search for temporary lodgings: a drive-in motel with a fast-in, fast-out garage, a rain-drenched roomboy who averts his eyes, a flight of stairs, and a small, dimly lit refuge on the second floor.

The motel room has the same smallish floor footprint as our house—so white and square that the walls disappear from our minds. But the glass in the windows has been painted dark grey and the curtains are heavy and filthy. The smell is a cheap construction of freon, cigarette smoke and car air freshener. Some music is coming from the ceiling speakers. Tinny and incomplete, like sounds on the roads we have passed. It feels as though we're on the very edge of our normal existence as husband and wife. But it also feels like we're dead center, with nothing but roads spiralling outward from us.

I fight an urge to rip the curtains apart and break the windowpanes open to the weakening light and the cold smell of falling rain. I want to break down the walls and feel the daylight that sits contentedly in the middle of our living room.

Days before my wedding day someone advised me not to ever look at my wife's naked body in its entirety. He warned that boredom would soon set in, and the marriage would be doomed. But as the dark gathers, there is nothing to do but look, nowhere to look but upward, where a mirror almost as large as the bed shows me her entire body, precisely framed and measured, like a picture frame around her. It's funny because we have no use for the mirror. I'm even half scared the bolts might give and send it crashing down.

Monica has a mole, a dark fleck like dirt on the rim of her downy navel. I look for a minute, looking not at her but at her in the mirror. I reach over and touch it. Moles are an accident of nature, with no real function or value. It seems painful to touch it, but she doesn't flinch, doesn't make a sound.

"So they'll still know its me when I die a horrible death. You know, my face might be mangled or something."

I read yesterday about that mountain of trash falling on the squatter community that surrounded it. Mothers went out of their minds looking and waiting for their chidlren and their husbands. The newspapers announced more than a hundred deaths, but unofficial reports placed the number closer to a thousand. After all, when entire families were lost, and there was no one to orphan or widow, who would come looking for them? I understood that it was difficult to search for the marginalized and the dispossessed, those exiled to live like trash among the trash.

There have been other disasters. Like that disco that burned to the ground, along with two hundred boys and girls, six or seven years ago. There were few survivors; the disco had no fire exit and the doors opened inwards. To a group of young man and women in panic, the room had become a tomb, their own bodies sealing it shut. Those who escaped carried third-degree burns and the raging memory of that night.

And years before that, there was the big earthquake, in the aftermath of which I met Monica, appearing from the anonymous crowd like a found object, a lost treasure.

Again I imagine the mirror crashing down on us, sparing my face but smashing hers, with shards of glass and metal. Even a little earthquake might do it. The bolts would be shaken loose, the threads would give, and the mirror would gape open, pointing its shiny jaw at her sleeping face. A second tremor, and the swinging angle would intersect with her sleeping softness. The impact is expectedly violent and the outcome, gruesome. Her face twists in my vision like morphing video. What can I do? The mirror invites such visions.

I try to feel how it feels being trapped for weeks under the broken glass and the rubble. I imagine I would survive, barely, and my wife would not. Through the layers of crushed steel, glass and concrete I hear the faint sounds of rescue teams and telephone crews coming in and going away, their picks and shovels and boots tapping on the silence with the faraway sound of insects' wings. Even Juliana's voice, crying out for her mother through the ruins, would sound weak and almost imaginary. We would be too buried, too well hidden.

Meanwhile, Monica's hair becomes dirty wires, the eyes, arched and half closed, become dark slits full of blood, and the bow-shaped mouth, still with a trace of coral-colored lipstick, everts itself to become black gums and crushed teeth. As the evening comes her body, too, loses all color and turns dark and grey.

But the mole remains, a small round bump on a flat, featureless frontier. It is so dark and round that it replaces her face. In my mind it begins to have features, looking up at me, expecting to trust me. You can tell she's had a child because of the swell of her stomach and the fine lines across its convex face. Stretch marks. She's sleeping now, once again, exhausted from the long and looping trip. In the mirror she is completely naked, with a white blanket bunched around her and underneath her, its folds like a vast ridge of mountains and rice terraces, a network of roads and bridges surrounding her white, smooth flesh.

In the darkness I try to piece together, from memory, my first naked image of Monica—of Monica before she became mingled with me. I must start from ground level: the feet, small, her calves fluted, her thighs thick and smooth like white cement. The curve of her belly was gentle, and in dim light had curves small and infinite, before reaching her small upturned breasts, her narrow shoulders, the fluted bones and cables of her small white neck. And then I piece together color, first a foundation of white, then infinite shades of yellow, brown, and pale red, piecing her together like the jigsaw puzzle to which I would soon connect, and in which I and all my construction would submerge and mingle with the pieces. Soon, mere months later, we first made love, I would become lost in her, once and for all time. I would put my face on hers, and she would put her face on mine, slapping them on and on like fresh yellow paint, until old emotions grew into new emotions, like annual rings on a dead, sawed-off tree stump, or the widening circle of buildings, roads, bridges, towns emanating from Manila, the epicentre, buildings built on the ruins of other buildings, destroyed by earthquake, politics, fire, emotion, war, neglect.

On the day she walked out on me, I arrived at the site to see a small crowd of architects and activists gathered in front of the fence, yelling and pointing fingers at the demolition crew. I took one last powerless look at the Sky Lounge, the sure sweep of its letters, the curve of its glass face, its absolute fullness and decadence. It looked like the hull of a doomed ship on its maiden voyage. The bottle would swing and strike, the structure would move and the ship would sail, never to return again.

She is all of a sudden old, and she doesn't move. She's dead and I am useless, both of us paralysed as the imagined earthquake rocks back and forth, lulling the dream city to sleep. Even dream cities fall. They fall because they are cities. In my crumbling city, I look at her, my heartbeat faint. One day they'll blast the fallen walls and uncover our hiding place, brick by brick, hollow block by hollow block. If they ever find us they'll find us like this, still as stones. •

18

Procession

TODAY WE TAKE MANUEL'S BEAT-UP VAN AND HEAD FOR THAT OLD hotel near the airport. From there, the island is a short pumpboat ride away. The sea between is calm, flecked with foam and flying fish. The island sand is soft and cream-colored, cool and forgiving to the soles of the feet, even in the heat of day. We shed our clothes as soon as we reach the white beach face and we bare ourselves to the sun in shorts, bikinis, halters and cut-offs, occasionally swimming out into the sea in gentle arcs, skimming the line where the shallow cup of green borders the blue of deeper water.

After our swim, we run across the sand, laughing, pale, lean and happy. The six of us cram ourselves into the hazy mottled shape of a shady refuge, arms and legs lightly touching, and easily slip into an afternoon siesta. During our rest nothing moves, only the sun and the shadows. We rise only when the moon is on its way up, to return to the boat and the van.

In three days, it will be Grace's eighteenth birthday. This year it falls on Black Saturday. Today she received a letter from her grandmother, Lola Alma, inviting all of us to her house in Sta. Ana for the Holy weekend and her birthday party.

The town is about four or five hours away. I've been there, though I've forgotten exactly when. The next morning we pack sheets and pillows and food for the road, and speed off just before the light comes. For two hours there is nothing on either side of us but streaks of raw, unbroken darkness, turning green and luminous with the sudden dawn. Bambi puts on a Chicane CD and we fall into a reverie. Suddenly, we're looking at the sky, bright and unfolded before us.

Manuel drives and I ride shotgun. We're listing with the creaking body of the ten-year old van. Grace sits between us, shaking a leg to the trance music. Bambi is behind us, asleep, and Manuel, Eric and Ella are smoking and looking out the window.

20 Manuel's driving brings us to Sta. Ana in under three hours, which, as far as we can remember, is record time. A few kilometers after the welcome arch, the green is finally broken by houses, gasoline stations, police outposts; and finally, the town's cemetery, like white bones spilled over the side of a wide, green hill. Grace has fallen asleep again. Her thin dark hair is scattered over my shoulder. Her hands are strewn across my lap.

Another cement arch, and we're in the town proper, where the roads are narrow and crooked, walled with houses of grey cement and old wood.

"Where to now, Gracia?"

Grace stirs, lazily looks out the window. "Lola Alma's house is three houses from the church. You turn right at a big acacia tree into a driveway and it opens up into a compound."

Manuel puffs up a cloud of smoke and heads for a cross on a low dome, rising above the metal rooftops. Soon we reach the town's center, with the church and the town plaza strung with lights and paper bunting.

Lola Alma has always lived alone in Sta. Ana. Her sister, Teresa, Grace's maternal grandmother, moved down to Manila as soon as she got married. The only nearest relatives, Tiyo Serafin and Tiya Karen, passed away some years ago, leaving her to tend their corner of the family compound. "They say I'm the one who looks like her," Grace says, and I look at her and try to imagine her sixty or seventy years older.

"This is it, Manuel. You turn here." Old men and women follow us with their eyes. Young boys playing on the street pause to squint curiously. "It's the last house on the right."

The compound holds two rows of houses, huddled over a narrow driveway. Lola Alma's house is the smallest, hidden at the farthest end behind a wall of sad-looking trees. An old man is sweeping dead leaves from the grass. When we drive up to the house he glances at us with thick glasses and a pained expression on his face. Grace waves from the van and he manages a slow smile.

"I thought you said your lola lived alone?" Manuel asks.

"That's Manong Carpio, the caretaker."

"Doesn't seem like he's capable of taking care of anything," Manuel quips.

"Well, they say he's been looking after the house ever since."

We alight quickly, uncoiling ourselves in the midmorning sun. Manong drops walis tingting and dustpan and disappears into the house. He returns silently with Lola Alma. From how I remember her: she looks the same, like any other

21

grandmother, stooped, wrinkled, trembling but always smiling. Grace greets her with genuine enthusiasm and makes a weak explanation for her mother's absence. I am surprised to find that her grandmother still remembers me. The last time was just Grace and me and we were just passing through on the way to a research site for our History class. We were just friends then, freshmen.

Lola Alma reaches out and I bend down and offer my cheek for her to kiss: a warm, fragrant, bony moment of contact, marked by a sharp sniff, as though she were smelling for drugs or sucking the life out of me.

Lola Alma's house is everything we expected. It's old and haphazardly decorated, smelling of dust and the dry air. Manong shows us around as Lola Alma and Grace catch up on old times in the living room. The kitchen opens up into a small farm. On the second floor are the bedrooms, one for the boys and the other for the girls, with a single bathroom in between. At the end of the hall is Lola Alma's room. At the other end, a wide balcony looks over fields and rooftops.

Manong Carpio retreats downstairs, leaving us to explore rooms that are full of thick, still air. We unload our stuff and open the closets. One contains old beddings and heaps of old clothes. When we open the other we are greeted by a man, frozen stiff, glaring at us with big eyes.

Bambi shrieks in horror. I look a little longer and realize it is the statue of a saint, with the posture and proportions of a department store mannequin, wrapped in clear plastic.

Bambi can't bear to look at it. She slams the closet door shut and lets out a nervous laugh. "What is that for? Why do they put it in a closet?"

"That's for tomorrow," Grace explains as she walks in. She's changed into a halter top and short shorts. "Each family sponsors a saint. On Good Fridays they take it out for the procession on the river."

"Gives me the creeps," Ella whispers.

"You should see Saint Ignatius. They make his statue ride a real horse."

"Fuck!" Bambi exclaims, then snorts in laughter.

We head downstairs and visit the small backyard farm, where Manong is busy preparing for the birthday celebration. He is sitting on a low stool, bent over a pail heaping with small dead birds. He is pulling feathers of the little rubbery bodies. A small pig is tied to a post, nuzzling the mud. Smoke wafts from the remains of a nearby fire, its red embers glowing with the stray breezes.

Manong Carpio speaks randomly, to me or anyone who'll listen. Sta. Ana is a miraculous city, having remained largely untouched through the war. The bombs fell harmlessly in the surrounding fields. What the town did attract was money, with the Chinese settling in during peacetime, setting up businesses around the town square, and with Spanish-Filipino families building big resthouses in the quieter corners of town. Even poorer families found room, setting up shops and small restaurants in between.

By the afternoon there is nothing left to do. Lola Alma has disappeared into her room for a nap. Eric puts on Bob Marley. But we're still restless.

Not far from the house is a river, thickened by mud from the mountains. We can see it from the balcony, a faint, glistening line at the edge of town marking the border between houses and the dark shapes of the forest and the mountains beyond.

As we walk through Sta. Ana the townfolk look at us and immediately know we're from the city, most likely by our schoolgirl Taglish, our city strut, our sunglasses, our bright colors and cross-trainers.

The part of the river bank we reach is the outer curve of a sharp bend. The water rolls quietly and curls around rocks and roots of trees. A little farther down, the river is spanned by a small wooden bridge that leads us into a thick growth of trees. We follow the trail as far as we can. Manuel uses a bolo to cut through entanglements of vines. We turn our handkerchiefs into bandanas. We cut our faces on the brambles and see nothing but trees and rocks and pools of dirty water. On the second hour Bambi begins to complain of fatigue and exhaustion.

To distract her Manuel and I sing an old song, "Balong Malalim" by the Juan dela Cruz Band. We don't know all of it so we sing just two parts, the first verse and the chorus. Soon everyone is singing. The rhythm of the song matches Manuel's hacking cadence at the head of the line.

Eric's voice cuts through our song, now in its third reprise. "I think I saw a clearing over there. I think if we go this way we'll get there."

The song is ended, the trail is renegotiated and Manuel's bolo picks up the pace. Soon enough, we come to the end of the bush, and reach a small bare area, covered only by tall grass and sudden sunlight, its silence silencing us in turn. Eric rolls a couple of joints and we feel our muscles relax and hear the sounds of the forest return. Grace sits next to me, her long white legs drawn up in the grass. The skin of her face and neck has reddened and her lips are parted with exhaustion.

We spend a couple of hours in the clearing, smoking, talking and laughing. Then we take the path back to the edge of the forest. When we reach the bridge it is almost evening. Our voices are drowned in the sound of crickets.

When we reach the house, Manong Carpio is already cooking dinner. The old woman is watching a soap on TV. The gang takes turns showering in the one bathroom. I go in after Grace, and as I enter I smell her body and feel her heat, closing in on me, sucking me in.

When I come out the table has been set, with fried chicken, steamed fish, monggo, dried fish, sukang tuba and brown rice. There is a bottle of red wine, Coke in a green glass pitcher, and for afterward there is leche flan on a raised dessert plate. There are also pineapples, oranges, mangosteen, fresh bananas in a basket. In a glass bowl there are more bananas, chilled in sweet, heavy brown syrup.

The old woman eats very little and talks a lot. She speaks of the river as though it were still the highway where all commerce flowed and from which all village order radiated. Tomorrow it will be filled with procession boats carrying the saints to the church.

When she speaks of neighbors or cousins or friends she remembers energetic young men and women in the place of the old, the sick and the dead, suspending them in time and place, tracing their origins before they came here before the war, when her small farm was still a garden, and the river and the forest were extensions of her backyard. It's old people talk—about the old town, the old time, when everybody knew everyone else and everybody was related to everyone else.

After dinner and dessert, our breaths taste sour and sweet, and our fingers are stained from the mangosteen and smelling of dried fish and vinegar. Lola Alma pours coffee and tells us about hearing the first bombs drop, a few days after the retreat

25

of the USAFFE, among them Lola Alma's first love. "A soldier, of all things!" Grace says.

Lola Alma is quick to defend herself. What else was there, anyway, during the war? But this one was different. "He was a doctor—a surgeon. Captain of his detachment. In the army they make you captain if you're a doctor."

Victor Jones was an American mestizo who waved to the nurses as he drove through the plaza in his USAFFE jeep, but always reserved a special, secret smile for her as he rode past the compound.

"We had big open-air parties in the compound. He was there in almost every gathering because he was a friend of a friend. Or someone's cousin, I think."

Ella grins. "So, 'la, did you get anywhere with this guy?"

"Well, we danced!"

We erupt into laughter.

"He was handsome. He had an American father who I think had moved in at the turn of the century, to start fresh. And maybe a mother with Spanish blood. Doc was tall and he had eyes that were bluer-than-blue, that seemed to look straight at you wherever you stood."

Before anything could happen, Dr. Jones disappeared, along with the rest of the USAFFE, just before the Japanese trucks rolled into Sta Ana. Lola Alma thinks he might have gone to the mountains, to fight with the guerillas. They needed doctors more because they saw fighting everyday. He never returned. Soon after that, her sister—Grace's grandma—got married. To a soldier, too.

After dinner, Manuel and Eric secure some gin, rum and lime juice and we sit on the balcony. Manong Carpio brings a guitar and some leftover fried chicken and earns his place in

26

our circle. We hear more stories from the old man about Japanese times. He tells us of how the Japs flooded the town with tanks, trucks and hundreds of footsoldiers. They gathered all the townfolk in the plaza, made a few announcements in Japanese, English and Tagalog. Rules were set, boundaries were laid, and examples were made of a few unfortunate men.

Manuel lights the last of our joints and passes it around. Manong Carpio takes a drag, coughs and chuckles a little bit, and places his tumbler on the floor and clasps the soles of his feet. He laughs a little more, and thanks Manuel for the treat. The sound of crickets is everywhere around us.

There was no procession during the war. When the troops came to the compound they ordered everyone out to the inner road and went through the houses one by one. They kicked open doors and ransacked closets and cupboards. They slashed paintings, ripped clothes. They took radios and record players. They even broke the cooking and bathing pots. But the statues were buried deep in the earth or under heaps of mulch and pigfeed.

By four in the morning Eric and Manuel are sprawled on the floor. Manong Carpio is nowhere to be seen. The moon is still full and round but the sound of the crickets has stopped. Grace lights a cigarette for us to share. We speak in smoky whispers. She looks up at the darkness, thinking and remembering.

Grace can't recall when she first met her grandmother. She remembers feeling very close to her, during the summers she spent in Sta. Ana. She tells me how the town was the same then.

She shifts her body and slides a leg over me. She sticks the half-spent cigarette in my mouth and closes her eyes. I look at her as she relaxes and her smile unclenches. I murmur into her ear, invite her to walk with me. We slip down the stairs, unbolt the door and step out of the house in shirts, shorts and slippers. The night is hot, but on the rare breeze, I can smell her skin, her sweat, a clean sharp smell coming off her neck and her hair. In the spaces between the breezes we hear the soft, flowing sound of water.

The town is quiet now, the streets half-lit by lamps that are too far apart. The moon fills in the blanks, along with our spotty daytime memory. As we retrace our steps through the town I hear her slow slim thighs rubbing against each other and the soft slap of her slippers, taking long strides in the dark. I can feel the sweat on the palm of her hand. Our pace gradually picks up, and soon we reach the blind bend. At night it seems more violent, its bank vibrating as it tries to contain the curving rush of water.

Grace stands trembling on the trembling ground, shaken by the darkness and the chaotic landscape. I reach for her, part her hair, kiss her on her feverish nape and whisper words into her skin. She turns to face me and we kiss.

On our way back we pass a group of men sitting in a tight circle over bottles of gin, looking at us with glassy eyes. One of them gives another a half-smile, throws his cigarette to the ground and shouts something at me.

I freeze and my shoulders tense, but Grace pulls me forward. We pick up our pace until we're running fast and hard, the sounds of our slippers tight and frantic and their growing taunts snapping at our heels. "Old men—they're harmless!" she shouts, grinning. Her hand grips mine tightly. As we run I catch a flash of her teeth in the moonlight: she is smiling, laughing even, quietly and breathlessly. Soon we lose our slippers and sprint the rest of the distance without them, feeling the pavement hard on the balls of our feet. By the time we reach the compound we are both laughing like maniacs.

We reach the refuge of the front yard, the foyer, the upper floor and the empty boys' room. On the eve of her birthday we are aching with fear and want. Our bodies slip and slide over fabric and wooden flooring.

The next morning, Lola Alma asks me to walk her to church. Manong Carpio, she explains, is busy preparing for the procession.

Like many old women, she has a clear memory of the past and a spotty image of the present time. As she leads me down their street past the rusty gate of their compound, she tells me to me how everything was laid out differently during the war. The basketball court was once a tiled area with gazebos and trellises lending shade in the hot afternoons. Where the columbarium now stands, there was a little garden with green paths between the gravestones. She makes a litany out of old people, people I have never met and who are long gone: Tiyo Filo, Tiya Bebeng, Tiyo Karo. And Pandoy, Nonoy and Ben who are in Daly City still waiting for their Veteran's pension, their American citizenship.

"My feet, my joints, my insides.. All of them ache now," she says. "The older I get, the more I feel every part of my body."

By now we are at the gate of the churchyard. The church bell is ringing and the townfolk are arriving for the mass.

"You're lucky, you know. Such a handsome boy. With your whole life ahead of you, with everything you want around you."

I am sweaty and slightly out of breath from the walk and from her weight bearing down upon my arm. Before entering

29

the church she turns to give me that old woman's kiss, and I'm afraid she might pick up Grace's scent from my cheek and my mouth.

LOLA ALMA TELLS ME THAT WHEN THE AMERICANS FINALLY CAME, AT the end of everything, they were welcomed like they were angels, like gods. All the big wooden saints that survived the occupation were dug up and brought out, and the Sta. Ana priests and elders decided to hold the procession ahead of time, rounding up all the small boats and rafts the town could salvage.

In the morning, we take places among the thick morning crowds at the river bend. Manong Carpio said this was the best spot to watch from, where the boats move slowest as they negotiate the shallow turn. By the time we get a good view half the procession has passed.

"There's our guy!" Bambi says.

We don't even know who our saint is. But he is there, standing proud and broad-shouldered in his boat, protected from the sun by Manong Carpio, who stands behind him in a long-sleeved shirt, shiny dark blue pants and leather shoes, holding up an umbrella over his wooden head. Lola Alma is beside him, freshly made up, her hair in a tight bun.

The statue's skin is freshly polished, his cheekbones and lips pinkish, with the kindest, gentlest doll's eyes and a trace of a smile.

"He's so gwapo!" Ella exclaims.

On the next day awake early, to loud squealing sounds from the backyard farm. When we get there the pig is already dead, its young, bright red blood spilling at our feet. Mang Carpio greets Grace solemnly.

Throughout the afternoon the house is overrun by forgotten and distant relatives. Grace's birthday party has turned into a homecoming of sorts. The rest of the gang is exiled to the balcony, where Marley is playing again and Manong Carpio has installed a table that duplicates the feast downstairs, complete with lechon, of course, and dinuguan, and the fried quail, with embotido and fried tilapia, and pancit for long life. There are bottles of beer in a cooler and a pitcher of Coke.

In the late afternoon Lola Alma brings us to the six o'clock mass for thanksgiving, and we come home to a simple supper of rice, dried fish and pork and beans from a can. At dinner's end Lola Alma thanks us and tells us she is too exhausted to get up early and bid us goodbye, so we make our goodbyes at the table.

In two weeks we are broke again and back at our island, skimming the water with half-naked, knifelike bodies. Today the sea is choppy, unpredictable, its dips and swells random and unplanned. Our pumpboat pilot, by way of apology and explanation, says that tomorrow, when we return, the weather will have turned and we will have a calmer crossing.

At night the island transforms into a cold, windswept, lonely place. Happy voices become dislocated in the blue light and turn absurd and lonely, like things spoken offstage, absorbed by the darkness and the waves. In the flicker of fires, faces become shiny, and bodies become tired and sandy. In the middle of the darkness someone lights a thick joint and we bob and weave with the waves, suddenly surrounded by molecules of sound, big and loud. Soon, the moonlight makes us glow with the light of ethereal beings.

31

Mosquitoes buzz over our head through the night, keeping us awake. We trade ghost stories. We're like islands ourselves, and the water erodes all there is around us. •

32

Thousand year eve

I HAD NEVER BEEN TO A RADIO STATION BEFORE, AND I WAS MILDLY shocked that it looked so ordinary. Even the offices adjacent to the disc jockeys' booths resembled those government agencies where you got your license or paid your taxes: a row of desks, clicking typewriters, worn-out, obsolete computers in a dirty beige color, a bunch of stonefaced secretaries, and a gaggle of people shuffling around and waiting in vague lines.

Off to one side, facing a corridor filled with people, were big square glass windows. Those were the disc jockey's booths. From small speakers perched above the windows came the sound of a woman's voice. In a corner of one of the windows was a little sign that said "On The Air"—just as I had expected it to be. The woman was weeping while speaking, and from where I stood, in the main office area, I thought I could see her figure in one of the booths, through the glare of reflections on the window.

The woman was calling for her missing mother. She was 68 years old, about 5 feet tall, with graying hair, and had worn a dress with blue flowers on the day she disappeared. They had gone to the zoo a week before. They had gone there because it was a Sunday and animals fascinated her. The old woman failed to show up at their prescribed meeting place. A three-hour wait ended in a search involving a gaggle of security guards. When closing time came—

The woman's voice was interrupted by the deep, booming voice of the announcer. I was surprised that it didn't sound tired, or hurried, or irritated, as I would most likely have been. It sounded just like that—exactly like that radio announcer we imagine in our head, a kind, dislocated voice overriding everything. With enough character but with a kind of indifference that comes from authority. It sounded as if it came from another world.

The woman then resumed, explaining that her mother had Alzheimer's disease. It was strange hearing the word "Alzheimer's" within the tones and textures of that voice, because I could tell the woman wasn't used to saying that word, and it sat in the middle of her sentences, perfectly enunciated, a newly built landmark that divided the past and the present. The term had been taught to her by doctors, experts, but it had surely never arisen between mother and daughter.

As I joined the people huddled outside the booth I could see into it. The booth was small, and the acoustic boards that lined the walls were covered with posters of movies and singers and bands. There were old memos and announcements. Wires sprung out from a stack of equipment.

The announcer sat behind a panel decked with buttons and sliding switches. He was wearing headphones and moving some of the switches. After a few moments I recognized him as a television personality. He hosted his own afternoon show. In the show he sat on a couch and fielded a string of guests. That show had a little oval inset in the corner that showed a woman performing sign language. I realized now that the show was a public service program—a televised version of the radio program he was running now.

And just like that television show, his guests took their turn in front of him, entering the booth and speaking into the microphone. Their voices emerged from the speakers above the window. After they spoke the host would speak. Then the booth door opened, a name would be called and someone from the hall would enter and sit in front of the announcer.

From time to time the sequence would be broken by a string of commercials advertising soap or insurance. Briefly, the sound would brighten and a jingle would play; after some minutes someone punched in the program ID, which was a short musical passage played on an organ that had the effect of a 1950s horror or mystery show. That was because the radio show was all about unsolved cases. Then, the announcements would resume.

One of the staff in the main office area called out my last name and I approached the booth. Before I could reach it the door opened and a little girl came out, tears streaming from her cheeks.

In my hands I tightly held a little piece of paper. On it I had scribbled some things that I imagined would be important. I had written out a long list, fearing I would forget something that turned out to be crucial information.

In the booth, the air smelled of cigarette smoke and damp air-conditioning. There was a little three-foot high Christmas tree in the corner, with light bulbs that blinked on and off and a little foil hanging that said "Happy Holidays." The announcer looked at me briefly and squinted at a clipboard. He gestured to a chair and took a long drag on a cigarette.

He called my name and I nodded. He switched on the microphones and announced my name on the air. All through

35

this I was turning the paper over and over in my hands until my hands and the paper had rubbed off on each other and shared the same color. I was folding and unfolding it, until I could barely read the pencil marks.

There was a microphone on a stand in front of me. I gripped the mike, adjusted its position and began to speak. I glanced down at the paper without looking, without reading, and spoke. I heard my own voice echoing through the studio as I began stringing together all the details.

My father, last seen New Year's eve, wearing a striped collared shirt, jeans and red slippers. Medium build. Black hair with white and silver streaks. 58 years old. Missing, lost, or kidnapped since New Year's Eve, four days ago. I was looking at the announcer, guessing when he would interrupt me with his silky voice.

He looked at me briefly, perhaps to see if I was done, and picked up the tail end of my fading announcement with a loud burst that was meant to add excitement to my case. The announcer looked at me as he spoke, and I recognized that he was giving me words of encouragement, telling me to leave my name and contact numbers on the master list outside. I felt, in that brief glance of his, that I found all comfort and solace. Then he switched his gaze to other matters: the control panel in front of him, the clock on the wall, the cue cards passed to him by an assistant. As he looked away he added that I would know in a few days. I stood up, gave the announcer a nervous smile, but he had turned to his list and was calling for the next guest.

In the main office area there was another line of people, all waiting to sign the master list, which was merely a set of clipboards arranged in alphabetical order. There was a woman at the desk who acted officiously, reminding people to hurry

36

up or fill in the proper blanks. After a while I noticed that the people respected her concern for order. After I filled in the blanks she offered me a Christmas greeting and reminded me that they would call me if there was any word. I stepped out of the office, past a fresh crowd that was gathering, and took a taxi to work.

Though it was the first day of work after the holidays, everybody knew that my father had gone missing. My wife and I had made sure to call every one of his friends over the past days. By New Year's morning, we had gone through the list of people we knew to know my father; by the next day we had gone even through those who didn't know him. It was quite an awkward thing, having to greet them for the holidays and then asking them if they had seen him, or heard from him. My father was a loud, gregarious man, and it was not unusual for him to call one of his friends, out of the blue, for a chat or a drink.

The office was still slumbering in the holiday spirit when I timed in, with only a handful reporting to work. My cubicle, normally unadorned except for a wall calendar and an appointment book, was cluttered with Christmas gifts from co-workers. I switched on my computer, mindlessly sifted and reorganized files, looked at the time, and made a few tentative calls.

When lunchtime came around, an officemate came over to my cubicle and invited me to lunch. I could tell his tone was guarded and unsure. I accepted the invitation with a voice that I hoped would not be so tainted with grief and exhaustion. I realized that the last time I had heard my own voice, besides the small remarks I had made to the taxi driver, was in the radio announcer's booth. Hearing my own voice now, exchanging pleasantries for the New Year's and agreeing to have lunch, seemed a strange and dislocating experience.

Whether it was because the holidays had drained all our funds or because we were in a somber mood, we chose to have lunch at the company canteen, a few floors down. Over lunch they asked me what had happened. I heard my voice once again telling them every detail of his disappearance, over the din and the soft music, with an accuracy that startled me.

After a small dinner, my father, my wife and my child went to bed to rest before the festivities. I sat in the living room watching TV and drinking beer. An hour before midnight, my father appeared and sat with me. He said nothing, merely coughing a little now and then. Some minutes later my wife emerged with the baby. She frowned at the sight of us sitting there and immediately went into the kitchen to prepare our Media Noche.

38

We had all wanted to go somewhere else to spend the holidays. My wife had wanted to take our one-year old child up to the beach in Ilocos, where her family would be staying, and Christmas and New Year's would be light and easy. I had made reservations at a hotel for myself and possibly a few friends, where I could sit and stew through the season.

My father and I took four worn tires from our garage and rolled them out to the street, piled them carefully in the middle, sprinkled a little kerosene and set the whole thing on fire. By that time our entire street was studded with tire bonfires and lined with people who had come out to watch the explosions and count the minutes.

That New Year's Eve was the millennium's eve. If anything, it meant that the explosions would be louder and the fireworks bigger and brighter. A half-hour away from midnight, the night sky was lit up with swirls of color, and from time to time, the swirls would reach down and ignite the street like lightning. On CNN they had followed the celebrations as the stroke of midnight crept across the world, jumping from country to country, showing an assortment of cultural celebrations and fireworks. They had been doing this since early evening, and by the time it was almost our time, the whole thing had begun to weigh heavily on me. My wife was still in the kitchen with the maid, preparing the New Year's Eve dinner. There were only three of us living in the small apartment, but my father always had visitors coming in after midnight, until the morning hours. By dawn our living room would be filled with old men, and the smell of old men, and the smell of cigars, cigarettes and liquor. I decided that after the midnight celebrations I would retire to my study and do some reading.

Because it was the millennium, we had stocked up on more fireworks than ever—and more than was necessary. By five minutes to midnight, the whole street was filled with fire and smoke. My ears were ringing and a thick fog of gunpowder smoke hung in the air. My father had changed from his pajamas into a striped, long-sleeved shirt and jeans. This was all protection—he always loved to stand close to the fire and toss in the fireworks, as though he were tossing garlic and onions into a frying pan.

When the fire had reached its full height, we sat on either side of our pile of fireworks—worth a lot of money if you ask me, but still not worth much against a sky that seemed like a sea of explosions. We tested our noise levels with a few firecrackers, and we were satisfied with the volley of small explosions they made, echoing back and forth against the high walls of our neighborhood fences.

As the firecrackers split open in the fire my father looked at me and said something I could not hear. By this time the explosions on the street had risen steadily into a continuous barrage. My father stood up and gathered an armful of big rockets. I was looking at my watch, counting down the seconds. I shouted for my wife to come out for the big bang, but she merely looked at me through the living room windows. The baby was crying hysterically from all the noise.

From the corner of my eye I thought I could see my father walking up the street, picking a path among the flare of fountains, the shockwaves of homemade bombs, and the sibilance of rockets shooting into the sky. I was seeing this from the corner of my eye; I didn't bother to call out to him because, thinking harder about it, I had believed all along that it wasn't him, it was someone else walking down the street. As the night turned to midnight and the sky and the street erupted into each other I looked around our bonfire for my father. When the next lull came, several minutes later, I realized that he had gone.

Is there any story that hasn't been told? Everything's been told, and told better. At the radio station there was a man who was calling out to his older brother who had neglected to send money from Kuwait, where he worked as an engineer. There was an old woman who cried for justice for her son, who had been raped and beaten to an inch of his life,, and whose pulverized jaw could not even accommodate a whisper of the name of his attacker. Wherever we go, there are other stories, other mysteries, wherever we go.

They had mysteries like this day in, day out, at the radio station, at the police precinct, at the barangay hall. In fact, all these places and cases so closely resembled one another that the pictures of the dead and missing, the telephone numbers

40

to call and the people to ask for on the phone, these names and things all melted into each other and began to look the same. Every 68-year-old woman stood five feet tall, had graying hair, and wore a flowery dress. Every old man looked the same.

In the taxis I rode, the radios were constantly tuned to the AM band, where the mystery show aired in the mornings and in the afternoons. Occasionally, breaking news came through the airwaves, involving phone calls from lawyers offering help or concerned citizens reporting the whereabouts of those lost and those who had run away. There were agencies and offices and even individuals out there who concerned themselves with the lost and the disappeared and the uncollected. I had earlier tried to solicit their help, but they told me the sheer volume of their clientele meant I might be attended to in many weeks' time. At that I resolved to do my own searching. By the end of the second week my father was still missing and I had almost grown desperate, but decided that it would be too late to go back to the help agencies.

My wife had delayed her move to Ilocos for the meantime. Whenever I got home, often very late after long hours at work and a slow, thoughtful reconnaissance around our neighborhood streets, I would be mildly surprised to still find her in her room, sleeping with the baby in her arms. I would sit and watch TV in the living room and discover that the persevering presence of my family had a difficult, grating character. By that time I realized I had owed her more than I could ever hope to repay and repair.

During those moments I agonized over the unanswered questions. Was my father, in fact, dead, killed at midnight by an explosion? I imagined a stray bullet falling from the sky, or a rocket veering off course to strike my father's slow-moving

41

figure dead center. But I shrugged off these possibilities as too impossibly fantastic. Surely the key to my father's disappearance lay in circumstances less spectacular.

I also reflected briefly on whether my father might have been the victim of a crime, such as an assassination or a kidnapping. I took to scouring the papers for any news of salvagings and unclaimed corpses. I was thankful for finding no such news, and decided that such a savage crime could not happen to my father. We were not exactly rich folk, and my father did not maintain a high position anywhere. If he was anything, he was simply and merely my father. It would have been a case of mistaken identity.

Still, I went to a newspaper to report it. A reporter asked me about the incident and, tired from the nth telling, I merely rattled off the details into his dictaphone. You forget the meaning of words the more you say them. But as I recited them I imagined the numbers and the details would bring my father from the void and contain him. I felt like a magician, a medicine man, uttering a spell composed of strange words, a litany of broken Latin that had to be repeated again and again, ad nauseum, until my familiar agreed to appear.

In a few days a small article appeared in the broadsheets, repeating my words, tucked under the bigger news of the current political expose. It also appeared in the tabloids, where it graced the pages where the small, sensational crimes of the day were reported.

More than once, the thought occurred to me that he might have faked his disappearance, that he might have walked away from our disintegrating life and marriage in order to save it. Or that he had turned an old pair of eyes upon himself and, seeing an old man growing older and unneeded in his son's household, decided to skip town and join his old gang in a journey to points unknown. After all, I seemed to remember that he had a thoughtful look in his eyes on the night he disappeared. Such possibilities lay open and waiting before me as I sat in my living room, looking at the news on TV and pondering my next move. I knew that such possibilities were very clear to my wife. After all, she had known my father all these years and she had come to know everything he was, as much as she knew everything about his son.

It was becoming an unsolved case. I remembered the organ stinger from the radio show and the woman at the radio station who had lost her mother at the zoo. I remembered hearing of old men and women going missing for days, even weeks, and I could see these old folks wandering from bus stop to bus stop, sleeping at the foot of buildings and begging for food. I imagined that after a while, they would have to build an entirely new life for themselves, without previous memories, like babies born to a new world.

43

It was at that time that I thought of summoning other, metaphysical means. A friend of a friend knew of a medium who specialized in lost items, and, wondering whether my father would count as a lost item, I contacted him. This time I was asked to bring a personal item of the lost individual. I could not bring anything very substantial, since my father had brought his wallet, put on his only cap, worn the watch I had given him many years before, and taken his only pair of shoes with him. I only managed to present a very old pair of bathroom slippers to the medium, who seemed to cringe at the sight of them.

The medium himself was an old man who wore a dingy robe whenever he performed his "readings." He clucked his tongue and declared that the item I had brought would certainly not do much, but added quickly that he would try, slapping down a deck of worn-down Spanish cards on the table. He made reshufflings and rereadings and offered several vague guesses about my father. Then he glared at me and decided that the old man might not be in the realm he was searching, or that he could be eluding his third eye. For a fee he agreed to perform periodic searches in the ethereal plane and assured me that if my father wanted to contact me, he would find a way.

True enough, that night I dreamt of finding my father. I dreamt that it was a clear night, like the night he disappeared, except there were no fireworks, nothing in the sky, not even the moon or the stars. In my dream he wanted to return and to signal his intention he lit the fireworks he had brought with him. Each rocket burned perfectly and burst perfectly in the night sky, exploding cleanly, like five exclamation points.

44   In my dream world the phone rang: "We've found your missing relative." I dressed quickly, feverishly, even forgoing my pants and socks. But when I arrived at the station to claim him, they showed me a different old man, sitting in a chair, sipping Coke from a small plastic bag. On the table beside him lay a half-eaten sandwich. In dreams, it seems, food is always half-eaten and everyone, most especially the dreamer, is almost always half-dressed. In dreams there are only half-discoveries. In dreams we expect to be tricked and are constantly jumpy, awaiting the strange twist or the inevitable fall. In the event of the latter, even a peaceful death is denied us, and we awake, sweaty and eyeballs still moving. As we spend the first waking moments trying desperately to remember our dream lives or wondering if a death in dreams provokes our real deaths, everything is soon forgotten and we move and live in the natural world.

The morning I awakened to was bright and clear, with the sounds of my wife and child in the next room.

I had dinner with my wife on the eve of her departure for Ilocos. She had prepared a simple meal, spare but thoughtfully prepared and accompanied by wine, as we had always had in the beginning. We did not speak at first, but after a few minutes I stammered a few compliments about the meal and thanked her for her support during the whole affair. I didn't know myself whether I was talking about my ordeal or the seven-year marriage. She smiled and as she spoke I could see in her eyes a new clarity and a great hope for her future and the future of the baby. Still, I was foolish enough to imagine that her pity for me and my continuing predicament would compel her to stay. Over coffee she gave me her contact numbers and e-mail addresses and offered an open invitation to visit.

Some weeks later I found myself at the radio station again, taking my place in the line across the booth. I looked at the announcer expectantly, to see if he remembered me. He didn't, of course. When it was my turn to speak, I discovered that time had rubbed the details down to an old, dull, unremarkable list of descriptions that could have matched anyone's. I might have been describing the old stranger I had dreamed of. I might have even been describing myself thirty, forty years later.

I imagined my own voice filtering through the mesh gate of the microphone in my hands, transported through the wires. I imagined it bursting from the overhead speakers like fireworks, bouncing off satellites, picked up by radios and skimming off the minds of listeners, sitting in their cars and their afternoon reveries. •

Rest stop

THE SNOW HAS BEEN BUILDING UP, GRADUALLY, FROM A SOFT AND pleasant fall for the coming holidays, into a growing drift, into what the man on the radio says will be a blizzard in no time.

I'm still far from the city and miles away from the next town. There's a rest stop a couple hundred yards ahead. I take the turnoff and park the truck under a tree.

The rest stop offers everything I could possibly need. There's a small gas station, a bank of restrooms, a cafe and a grocery store. During easier weather it would be run over with Range Rovers or compact German SUVs, top-heavy with luggage and skiing equipment. Today there are only two or three other cars in the parking lot, each of them growing a mantle of snow.

I let the engine and the heater run while I double-lace my shoes and put on my parka over my sweater. Under all this I am already wearing thermal underwear and a shirt. I put on a woolen cap and dare a look at the rearview mirror. My eyes are scrunched up into a frown. Through all my years of driving around in America I never got used to all this cold.

I sit in the truck for a moment and contemplate the thirty yards between the car and the door. I turn off the engine, stuff the keys into my jacket pocket and flip my collar up. The heat fades quickly and the windows fog up. My breath comes out in little clouds. I open the car door, plant a foot outside, and then another, and then lift my body out and close the door behind me, all in one passably fluid motion. I stuff my hand in my pocket and squeeze the autolock button as I hustle to the door and into the grocery. All this happens in a kind of slow motion, and all sound is drowned in the growing howl of the snow and wind. My knee has been slightly banged by the closing door and there is a dull ache in my shoulder, caused, I guess, by all my twisting around to pull my parka on.

The place has been made to resemble a ranch or a log cabin. It's warm and made to look friendly, with handmade signs announcing daily specials in pleasant block handwriting. I slip off my gloves and my parka and pick up a shopping basket.

As I turn into an aisle, my basket briefly brushes with another, then firmly locks mesh. I mutter an apology: "Pardon me." I find myself face to face with Ditas, her hair short and curly, tinted a light brown. She's in a checkered brown coat, over a blouse with the collar up. I remember my scowling face in the mirror and take my cap off. We'd look good in a picture, taken right now, with matching colors and warm, spontaneous smiles.

"Soy," she stammers. "Soy! When was the last time!"

She knows it's been long too, but forgets how long it's really been. The last time was a fund-raiser at the Plaza Hotel back home. That was a few years after college. She was with the party of the guest of honor. I was with the press contingent.

47

At the party I spoke to her for the first time since school, under the pretext of doing research for a feature story I was writing.

I was brimming with confidence then, charged with excitement about going to America. A cousin of mine had arranged for a position for me at a dental supply factory in Jersey. The position was officially "jobber." I soon found out it meant seventeen years' worth of long drives, all across America, from coast to coast, through the heartland, and sometimes even upward into Canada.

So I tell her how long it's been, without all the sordid details, dressed in a rough estimate: "Twenty, twenty-five years—at least!"

"Well, you look great, Soy," she says, her tone perhaps a little forced.

"Right." I almost raise a hand to smooth my hair.

"Oh, you look okay. Getting old in all the right places, I guess. Not like me, huh? All fat and ugly."

I give her my protestations. As we line up at the checkout counter I look at her basket: saltines, apple juice, green grapes, marmalade and a small wedge of cheese. I slide my stuff over before the total is punched. After a brief argument she agrees to let me pay for her basket, plus mine, which is just two bottles of wine, frozen cheesecake and some toiletries.

I cannot help but notice, though, how she's grown a bit smaller. I have heard that age does that, among many things. But factoring my shrinkage, I'm still a head taller than her. I am now at fifty-something and peg her age at about the same. However, I'm thinking it could be my imagination. Over here, we're smaller than most people. I'm used to doing business with big Americans, with their big bodies and big voices.

48

At the café we order two big cappuccinos and a slice of chocolate pie.

"So what are you doing now?" she asks.

"Oh, this and that. Rediscovering things. I've decided to go back to writing. Do you remember that I used to write?"

My question comes and goes unanswered, but she smiles at me, and I think it's a smile of vague familiarity. Years ago, before America, I was winning contests and publishing in local magazines.

"And how is America treating you?"

"Okay, I guess. I'm well-fed, as you can see." I afford an expansive gesture. "I'm worth one Social Security number and a Democratic vote."

She smiles and gives me the once-over for the second time that day. For the umpteenth time all in all, I guess. In high school and college we were batchmates, but always in different classes and certainly different gangs. She played badminton at the Polo Club on weekends and flew to Hong Kong every six months to go shopping. I was one of those guys who had neither the money nor the nerve to court her. I was smug, though. I pretended that my choice of wardrobe—T-shirts, jeans and sneakers—was a matter of simplicity. Her reaction was quite as simple, and full of the smugness of the real kind: a once-over, a twice-over, and then she probably never gave me another thought.

"How's your wife?" she asks, as if she has caught me remembering. "I mean, I assume you're married, right?"

"Well, I *was* married," I say, showing off my ring finger emphatically, where I imagine a permanently untanned stripe. "To my ex-wife."

49

Most every separated man I know says "ex-wife" with a kind of relish, like it's a place they've been to, like Miami or New York and they'll tell you about it if you like, or even if you didn't like. My wife and I were married, for all of four short years, without children, and with me spending most of my time on the road. To be honest, I can hardly remember anything, good or bad. Maybe talking about it on a Sunday morning, to a person I knew even before my ex-wife, makes me a little more thoughtful than usual.

Maybe, also, it's Ditas' accent: old and comfortable music to my ears, a Filipina kind of English, alternately hard and soft, hitting the words right in some places and not quite right in others. It moves me just to see her mouth moving and saying those words, speaking this way, to me of all people.

My turn comes to ask.

50

"How's your husband doing? Alfonso, right?"

"Ponso's doing okay. His business is holding up—he still owns that chain of pawnshops back in Cebu, plus lots of other little things. Remember Cebu, Soy? When was the last time you were there?"

"Haven't been there in ages. Not since I was there last with you. Not since I was there when you were there, I mean. At the Plaza Hotel near the top of that hill. It was a charity dinner, remember?"

She was in a polka-dot dress, and stunned the crowd when she turned and showed her bare back. She arrived with the son of an important Cebu businessman.

I was writing a feature on "provincial beauties." I interviewed her on the hotel balcony, right outside the ballroom. She ordered three or four cocktails for the interview and smoked Virginia Slims while we spoke.

"Those were wild times, Soy. I still remember them, and laugh about them sometimes. "

That businessman was Alfonso. She married him some years later, in a ceremony that warranted a page's worth of photos in the Inquirer's society section. Some time later I heard rumors that their marriage was over, that it had only been for show that they were still together at weddings and cocktail parties.

In the window behind her I can see that storm has let up a little bit during our conversation. The café is deserted, save for the waitress and the cashier and a young couple cooing to each other at the far end. Through the windows the landscape is so quiet and empty it looks frozen. Acres of white snow stretch into the distance.

"It's so peaceful here, Soy."

"It's everything here. I always take it for granted, you know, until I look at the Filipino papers or hear about another kidnapping or another government scam. They say the peso's still going down, and there's no end to violence in the South."

"Haay, you're right, Soy." She puts her cup on the saucer, brings a pale hand to her chin.

"Aren't you scared?"

"Well, I am scared as scared can be. And everything just seems to work here. My son seems happier, more at ease. We went malling the other day and everything seemed to fall into place. I saw things in another light."

"You bet!" I say.

Things fell into place for me, too. There were some rough spots, some tough times. I had a good marriage that made a wrong turn, but the divorce delivered sure and swift relief. I turned my life around, quit my job and even started writing

51

again: public relations articles for an environmental advocacy group. You'd need to hold down at least a dozen jobs like that back home to hold you up. And that would be barely.

I pay good rent on a nice enough apartment with a small view, with enough left over for movies and malls and the occasional evening at the card table. I even have enough money to buy a Ford 4x4, second-hand, off a couple who were moving to New York. It's a little worn around the edges, but it's a lot better than the old Honda. And it cuts a sharp figure with the women. They're also impressed, I think, by the fact that I can drive a stick, a talent earned hard as a college kid, over days of struggling with an uncle's old owner-type jeep. I'd get my chance at the wheel after school, in exchange for doing chores. I'd ground the transmission down until that old jeep was practically unusable but I had learned shift with or without the clutch pedal.

But I never learned to get up the nerve to talk to Ditas, who I saw everyday in school. I dreamed about her, about spending every spare minute of our time together, in the dorm and in the library, in the gym, even spending the night in the middle of the sunken field that lay at the center of our University, looking up at the stars. You see, in those days I wrote nothing but poetry, and even published some.

"So what do you do? How long have you been here?"

"Me? Oh, I just flew in. Only last week."

"A vacation, then."

"Well, you know how it is. One thing or another. The main reason is that my only son, Kaloy, has a medical condition and I'm having him checked here. That's why we're here, I guess, among other things."

"Medical condition." Politeness behooves me to repeat her concern. No, I don't know how it is, exactly: that condition, or any one of those other reasons she has for being here.

"Yes, unfortunately," she says. "Our doctors back home referred us to a specialist clinic around here. And you know what? When we went to the clinic I found out the specialist here's Pinoy too. All the way here in the middle of nowhere!"

"Yep, we make the best doctors. Just like men make the best chefs. And yes, we're everywhere. Look at me."

She chuckles at the lame remark, although I can see that part of her mind is still on her son. I ask her about how old the son is and she says he is twenty-two: an early age to have any sort of medical condition but then, with what the world is coming to now, it is hardly any surprise. Things come up from behind you and then you just learn to take things as they come.

53

"Well, it's—it's cancer," she reveals finally, and I can't say anything to that. I haven't had cancer in the family, not that I've heard anything about my family recently. At home there is only me. I don't know what kind of pain is involved, or how much it costs.

"Cancer," I solemnly repeat. I can see the storm's white turbulence picking up in the window behind her. I try to imagine what it might do to the truck, remembering the other cars I saw in the parking lot, smothered in snow beyond recognition. "That's too bad," I offer.

Under her coat, Ditas is dressed in an expensive-looking white shirt and jeans, and her short hair is accentuated by those light brown highlights every woman likes to wear these days. On that night she wore her hair in a French braid, the fashion of the time.

I put a ten-dollar bill on the table and get up to pull her chair out. I help her into her coat and she begins to argue, but I'm quick and decisive. I ask her if she needs a ride and offer to drive her around the countryside because she seems to need the fresh air. The houses in this area are beautiful and some are about a hundred years old.

"Oh, Soy," she says, and it can go both ways. But this time I don't take no for an answer. I grab her things with a quick smile before she can reach for them, and we walk outside and head for my pickup. I put my hand in my pocket and feel for my keys.

The storm has let up a little. I can hardly feel it now, but I know it's out there, gathering strength before it starts ripping everything up. Snow is quiet and friendly, but when it gets violent it causes water pipes to blow and freezes the homeless dead in their beds. It makes the roads slippery. I've seen a couple of smashups myself. In the last one there were even a couple of bodies. The cops pulled them out of their car and laid them out in the snow, side by side.

I had borrowed my uncle's jeep for that evening—I was kind of hoping for something right to happen. At the time the idea of America accepting me had given me such strength, such hope. From the balcony of the Plaza Hotel there was a view of the sea on one end, and on the other, low mountains of brown and green. That was my last good view of home. •

54

New wave days

SHE ENTERS THE CIGARETTE BAR, PARTING THE CROWD, AND MY FIRST thought is, haven't I seen her before, somewhere? She takes a seat at a corner table. A waiter whisks away her reservation card, opens a glass cabinet and plucks a pack from a stack of Marlboros. Her name is on a brass plate on the shelf. She doesn't speak, and doesn't appear to be waiting for someone. She is dressed in a silver top and pants.

The music at the bar is strictly New Wave. A Flock of Seagulls is playing "Wishing." The walls flash videos of the Cure, Kraftwerk, New Order, other bands I don't know or can't remember from stories from my father. It's after hours. The bar is packed shoulder to shoulder. The ionizers are working overtime to clear the smoke.

Why does she make such an impression on me? Let us say that I feel an impulse, a tiny electric prick of instinct that triggers in me a mild curiosity, a gentle push toward something I can't figure out. Sure, she is beautiful. In this part of town, gentle genetic tweaking makes all the women beautiful. But it isn't that. I can't quite put a finger on it.

The music seems to mean nothing to her, not even when they play a U2 anthem and the smoky, sweaty crowd goes wild. But when she lights up her Marl light I see a breath of pleasure flit over her face. When was the last time I was witness to such pleasure on a woman?

How odd, I think, as I light up a moderately priced filterless, that our kinship, our courtship begins around such vice.

FROM MY TINY FLAT IN THE UPLEVELS, MORNING SKIES ARE THE texture of brushed steel. My window looks out into the cleft between beds of clouds, a westward view, with the spires of other residential buildings faintly visible in the distance.

I call Paula's number. The beep comes on and I announce that I am coming over in two weeks to see our children. I'm not coming over this week because I'm doing something this weekend. "Message sent," a voice recites. It is a female voice, warm and synthesized.

Boredom pushes me to do something, to go somewhere, and I go to Thailand, where the worn-out wats await, rotting and sinking silently, their walls and towers half-buried in the hot earth. On my way to Ayutthaya, there are crowds of people at every bus stop. I try to take solace in the shade of broken stupas and at the feet of idols of dying religions, but even here there are hordes of students, honeymooners and backpackers. At the Wat Phra Mahathat there survives a celebrated row of fifteen stone buddhas, all with severed heads, but in the face of such violence posed so calmly and quietly, with joined hands, as though they had expected this to happen, hundreds of years after their creation.

The sunlight makes sightseeing a nasty, unbearable affair. Hot and hungry, I call the service for a restaurant. The voice suggests the Duangporn restaurant, just around the crowded corner. I am relieved to find that it is as quiet as a temple. I cannot remember ever being alone in a restaurant. I pile my pack and solar veil on a seat and look at the menu, written completely in Thai. It gives me a secret pleasure to find other languages still living in the quiet, hidden corners. The waitress, small and brown, is mechanical with her translations and explanations. I order two kinds of noodles, a vegetable dish and a Coke.

The glass door swings and it's the woman who walks in, fresh from the dangerous sunlight and the dry and dusty air. I know this, even before she lifts her solar veil to reveal her face, stricken with a pale, wide-eyed look, the look of a tourist, shy, inquisitive, almost stupid, all at the same time.

I am filled with a strange, liberating, paralyzing energy. Trembling as I sip my customary hot and sour soup, sweating from the long walk across ancient stone and earth, I look at her furtively, from behind my bowl. She is in a khaki-colored dress. I can see her shins, milky, shiny, vulnerable to the hot light. She seeks out the waitress, mutters something to her. She opens her pack, reaches into the bottom and retrieves two cigarettes. I imagine the kind of money or connections it would take to smuggle in two cigarettes through the airport.

She looks around, at the wide window behind me, at the hard, reddish sunlight and the lumbering crowd outside, and then locks eyes with me, very briefly. I struggle with all my might to break her gaze. Does she recognize me? Her eyes glaze over as she inhales. The cigarette end glows, she blows out a stream of smoke and a ribbon of pure satisfaction courses through her. The smoke is whitish grey, a sign that it comes

57

from pure tobacco, made more precious by its journey through her liquid mouth, her soft lungs, the delicate chambers of her nose.

I lose my rhythm in Bangkok. It is meant to be a paradise for antiquarians like me, but as I walk the streets and brave the market crowds I am constantly visited with the feeling that I am being watched and followed. On street corners I look around furtively, searching for telltale signs, plumes of contraband cigarette smoke, or the sound of footsteps, gracefully light but with a quick, purposeful cadence. I am sleepless in my midpriced hotel. I sit stonefaced in restaurants. No spice can bring tears to my eyes, no color can move me, no lissome prostitute can charm me. I ride to the airport early, and wallow in my thoughts as I wait for my flight home.

58

I HAVE COME ACROSS SUCH PHENOMENA IN MY READINGS. ONE OF the most memorable instances is chronicled by Krip Yuson, who wrote of a "doppleganger," which is German for "double self," that seemed to follow him wherever he went. Never mind that his double self was a religious leader of a self-made faith. Father Tropa dressed in white robes, walked barefoot and liked to sling a six-foot reticulated python over one shoulder. Krip Yuson would find himself in the same office building with him, at the same café, or even at the same bank. He would be depositing his writer's honorarium and Father Tropa would be making similar transactions.

At the time, which was before my time, Father Tropa ran a little-known program called "Fr. Tropa's Spaceship 2000 E.T." airing in the late evenings over one of the weaker free channels. Father Tropa postulated that in the year 2000, an extra-terrestrial spaceship would land and carry the righteous away to the utopia of another universe, a heavenly civilization far more advanced than our own. To Father Tropa being righteous meant walking barefoot and loving the forests and the seas as much as he loved his python and the forests and hidden waterfalls of his native Dumaguete City.

Father Tropa and Krip Yuson have since moved on, pythons have gone extinct, and the exploding population has crowded into every hidden place. Our dependency on forest and sea has gone, and while there are still no absolute signs of extra-terrestrial intelligence, we have huge, unmanned robotic spaceships, preprogrammed to mine planets and moons. But, apparently, strange coincidences and synchronicities abound, such as the phenomenon observed by Yuson and involving him and an unsuspecting Father Tropa.

When I get home I remember the children and call Paula. Instead of a beep, her response comes, "okay," in two syllables, followed by another voice in a warm whisper: "end of recorded response." That synthesized female voice again. I imagine the kind of woman that would make a voice like that, and if she were a real flesh-and-blood woman, what kind of messages she would hear over a day, or a month, or a lifetime. How many of the same messages would she have to listen to, over and over again, cloned across time and space?

The last time something remotely synchronous happened to me was when I bumped into my great-grandfather at one of those low-end malls in Davao. I was young then, still working. I was there for a convention, only in and out. I decided to kill some time before checking in at the airport. I instinctively told the cab driver to head for the nearest mall.

I almost didn't recognize my great-grandfather because he had grown so old. Perhaps also because I had forgotten what he looked like. But he recognized me, and gently collared me as I turned a busy corner, like I was a young boy. But perhaps to him I was young and feckless. I felt his weak grasp, turned, and saw that he was so old that he resembled an otherworldly creature.

Davao is a big city, but my great-grandfather had found me in a mall full of people. I was genuinely happy to see him—years later I recognize that some guilt was at work here. He was on his way to the bookstore. I went with him. I was curious because it was my first time to visit a bookstore. It was tiny, with space for only the shopkeeper and my grandfather and me, and it had the brown, acid smell of rotting paper. I treated him to a heap of sorry-looking pocketbooks, Westerns by Zane Grey and Louis L'Amour. He loved them both, loved all their books. It amazed me that one could write so many books in a single lifetime. I couldn't even imagine reading so much.

My great-grandfather told the children he was a cowboy in his younger days. He liked to remind us by walking in a bowlegged swagger. He wore his slacks low on his hips, and from behind he really looked like those cowboy gangsters in the movies. He would tell us stories about actual gunfights and surprise encounters, about lynchings and the law of the jungle. But when I knew him, he was already thinning out, turning into a transparent, worn-out waif. He was completely mechanical from the waist down, and the sun had degraded his skin into a stretched film. Only constant medication, organ implants and delicate nanosurgery kept him alive.

On weekends, there is no work, and what sustains me is my yearning to see my children and the memories of Paula waking me with the smells and sounds of cooking. I head for the city station, where the early crowds await the interisland train.

THIS TIME, IT SEEMS THAT I AM THE ONE FOLLOWING HER. AS I BOARD the train, I see the woman sitting calmly, almost directly across from me, staring at the middle distance, oblivious to the Sunday rush to the provinces. She has her hands in her lap and her fingers are laced together. It seems as if she's wary of the crowd, ordinary people, old men and old women, laborers in slippers, carrying sacks of merchandise, or produce. She is in a dress of what almost seems like real linen—white flowers in a field of blue.

She raises her eyebrows when she notices me and almost makes direct eye contact. The look of shock and recognition is sustained for a few moments, but I am quickly lost in the huddle of people. My own thoughts are whirling as I find my place among the standing crowd and reach for a handle. There is almost no room to breathe, no space for my satchel, heavy and bulging with gifts from my children.

The train makes a long stop at Bacolod, and I lose sight of the couple as the people shuffle and squirm their way out. A fresh crowd enters the train, and a few moments later, I hear the beep and that female voice calling from the ceiling speakers, in a warm whisper that cuts across the din: "Doors closing. Please mind the doors."

It takes eight more minutes before the train reaches Cebu station. The doors open and I let myself be swept by the crowd into the hot and briny air. Umbrellas are unfurled, solar veils unrolled, and I scramble for a taxi.

Paula is an economist who works for the Central Bank. Everyone in her uplevel building works in the same office. She chose government work because it allows her a four-day workweek and gives her more time for the children.

When we were still married I worked as a technician at a statistical firm. I managed the machines that direct the flow

61

of traffic from city to city, that drive the turbines and the engines, the same interconnected system that assigns airplane seats, plans vacations and compiles the television programs you're most likely to like. It's a complex, continuous, self-correcting process, perfecting itself over a number of years, adapting to an individual's evolving tastes. On a plane the machine always assigns me to a window seat because my skin is darker than normal and my vision is 20/20. Ten years ago I would always get aisle.

We had some good times, we shared some love. She was a woman of some intelligence. She understood some of what I was doing. But soon enough, cracks and white hairs began to show. The white hairs were ours—she assiduously dyed hers black, while I left mine sprouting from my crown like a spreading halo of clouds.

62   But the cracks, I confess, were all mine. They appeared on the delicate matrix I had formed around our love. She was always the practical one, while I had spent the last moments of our marriage, rediscovering the joy of reading. I spent most of my salary buying books in tiny antique stores and brought stacks of them into our already cramped apartment. It began to smell of paper, musty and acid-soured. Paula imagined it carried ancient diseases and would make the children sick.

That was the other thing that happened during my chance encounter with my great-grandfather. It awakened an obsession for reading—not just for the tatty Westerns and archaic spy-thrillers that were once fashionable with the old and distinguished, but for classical literature, the antique arts of fiction, theatre and poetry, works that held in their depths patterns of thought, and patterns within patterns. It thrilled me to find nested meanings and well-planned coincidences.

I met Paula during a population commission seminar, where everyone was being encouraged to fall in love and marry early. At the popcom center we give blood samples and cheek scrapings and the system works it out so that our search is narrowed down and we waste less time, less space.

They served snacks and beer. There was a New Wave band and everyone was dancing. Paula was seventeen. She spoke with a trace of Visayan she had picked up from her Cebuano mother. She knew the words to the songs because her mother was in a New Wave band. She liked the Go-Gos, Modern English and the B-52s. I was New Wave, too. My dad turned me on to Japan and the Lotus Eaters and New Order.

They seat us beside each other because they we have these things in common. By the end of the session we're harmonizing on "Melt With You" by Modern English.

The actuarial programs were right about our affinity, my virility, her fertility. What they failed to see was our failure, our lack of bravado, our resistance to the natural flow. We quickly became an anomaly of the times, arguing under the hot sun, polluting the air with our angry noise, infecting the harmony with our unease.

"Arrival at destination, time is ten hours forty-five," the female voice says, and the taxi's doors open at the foot of a skyscraper, to the noise of people and the sudden heat of the sun. Crowds await to board my taxi, and as when I enter the building there are long, unruly lines at the elevator bays.

When I reach Paula's flat the door senses me and recognizes me but remains closed. "The party you wish to visit is away," the voice whispers to me, and a small green light flashes in the eyehole. "You may record a message if you wish."

On the ride back I cannot find the woman. It feels strange, I almost feel incomplete.

I AM THRILLED BY THE IDEA THAT OCCURS TO ME OVER THE NEXT few days. I place a call to the popcom and, at the voice prompt, request for an anonymous search. I give details from memory: the name of the cigarette bar, her last name on the brass plate, her visit to Thailand.

There is no waiting, no discernible sound of files being accessed or databases being queried. The voice answers me as easily as though I were asking one of those Thai prostitutes their name. That the woman's name is Elena Chan, that flesh-and-blood woman whom I encounter now at almost every train, every shopping trip, every random turn I take. The voice patiently tells me her contact numbers and addresses. It breathes to me her hobbies and interests: archaeology, art, textiles and tobacco smoking. I am soothed by her cadence, her tones and her sibilance as she whispers above the crowd. Elena Chan is Filipino-Chinese, a businesswoman with interests in trading, freight forwarding and mining. The report is short but comprehensive. "Thank you for using this service."

Elena has the complexion of a flesh-colored pearl. Her flawless body seems to have been thawed from cryogenic chambers. Her skin, synthesized from the skin of those unborn. Her flesh formed whole and new, without trauma, without memory, to become the woman that she is now, needing no words to be wise and beautiful, needing only to be silent, glimmering on the edge of my vision, visiting almost every public place I visit, perfectly by chance.

Slowly, over the repeated chance encounters, Elena has ceased to be a stranger to me. I know her backward and

64

forward, and I know whether she is coming toward me on the sidewalk from a mile away, or sits several rows in front of me in a dark movie theatre. I am now familiar with the color of her arms, the movement of her hair, the shape of her smoke. I have grown almost comfortable with my obsession.

I never saw my great-grandfather again after I bought him that heap of pocketbooks. One day he ran into a freak accident on his way to the market. The jeepney he was riding lost its brakes, swerved to avoid a child on a bicycle and flopped like a fish on the main road.

But I remember him from his cowboy stories. He boasted that back in World War II they made him commander of a local guerrilla army. He was a vigilante. He and his men ambushed supply convoys and small encampments. They liberated small prison camps. For a while he had become the town hero, the one thing the Japanese feared. He took no prisoners. He would execute every Jap he found and report to his superiors that they had tried to escape. He had a past to defend us from. It was a past steeped in war and disease and violence, he would tell us. The words gripped us in silent terror, me and my seven brothers and four sisters, children of the new prosperity, a world where the golden path is prescribed for all.

I feel an inner eye open, and I see Elena and me, our paths inscribed and reinscribed on the same ground by invisible hands and invisible voices, those that have seated us at the same bar, in the same car of the same interisland train, that have sent us roaming around the same temple, our hungry spirits seeking comfort and meaning from the same silent stone.

Paula is not home again when I arrive for my next visit, but the door accepts my presence and opens to the sight of my children, sprawled on the floor playing videogames. I unwrap my presents for them: wooden replicas of the lost Buddha heads, rendered in the Ayutthaya style, with pointed crowns, elongated earlobes and the thin, closed eyelids of the enlightened. And as an afterthought, a present for Paula, who has never been to Thailand, a replica of the Buddha's hands, in shiny brushed steel, closed in a final acceptance.

At the shopping mall I try calling Paula again. The voice tells me the party is unavailable. The system picks up my location, my slightly raised blood pressure, perhaps my ancient fear and distrust of crowds, and in warm, reassuring tones, suggests refreshments and guides me to a nearby café.

At the café Elena sits with an old book and a half-empty cup of coffee. OMD is playing "Talking Loud and Clear." She turns her head to look in my direction, and I'm rooted to the spot.

It's like a Mexican stand-off, a showdown at high noon. She walks toward the door, toward me, until she's terribly, dangerously close, now close enough to shake my hand, now close enough touch my face. The possibility unnerves me. I see the individual strands of hair on her eyebrows, the pores on her face moist with sweat, the marks under her eyes, tired from the strain of the sun and the mass movements of the crowds all around us. I can almost smell her breath, a neutral smell, but with a trace of tobacco and something else I will not be able to know, not until I taste it on her mouth and skin, perhaps one day, when my fear is gone and I will be able to see Elena as she is, a gift, a prophet of joy and pleasure. While I am thinking this she moves past me, tucking her book into her handbag and disappearing into the crowd, but I know I will see her again.

Back at the apartment, overlooking a steel-colored sunset, I light a cigarette and linger in the delicious smoke, spiraling toward the ceiling, on the inescapable path of self-healing and enlightenment. •

67

Nilda

THE KISS WAS FULL OF TONGUE, AND ALL SENSATIONS MINGLED ON the tongue. It felt like a sliver of flesh from a stony green mango, one of many I plucked that summer from my perch on the lowest branch of the tree in our front yard.

My yaya Nilda stripped the skin off with a rusty old peeler and made deep parallel cuts with a knife, the blade making clean, bloodless wounds in the whitish flesh. She sat me down in the kitchen on a warm afternoon, my mouth wet, my hair and body hot and smelling of the sun. She handed me the knife, and I sliced close to the seed, with what force I could muster, so that in one sure stroke the slivers came away and apart, falling like white fingers into the palm of my brown hand. She prepared three kinds of dippings in round bowls: rock salt, sugar steeped in dark soy sauce, and red-brown bagoong. I dipped and brought the slivers to my mouth, tasting now the sharpness of crystal, now the sweet and salty mush, now the briny mulch, against the mango sliver, hard rind and tender flesh meeting teeth and tongue, making the inner cheek swell and pucker with pleasure.

During the kiss, we were sitting wet by the pool. She tasted my mouth with hers and pressed herself against me and I smelled the surge of pool chlorine, coming off clean and sharp from her skin. She slipped the straps of her bathing suit off and her shoulders were like white-wings. I looked down and saw her breasts, freshly peeled, small and pale, squeezed against my body.

It was the eighties and I was all of thirteen. My father, an attorney, worked for the government. He was tall, thin and handsome, but he was also tense and hunched, like he was listening for a signal or poised to make his next move. He had small alert eyes and wore his lips in a constant curl, ready to make the quick comment or deliver the hard order.

The dark suit was his trademark. I suppose he liked the way he looked in it, bigger and meaner, with the shoulderpads becoming his shoulders, the dark, shiny shell his skin and flesh. To cover his large ears, he styled his hair in a big bouffant. Moroy told me large ears meant a long life. From their size and the way they stuck out you'd think my father would live forever. To complete the look he wore a blank expression on his face that was so impenetrable it scared both acquaintances and strangers. But what really made him scary was Moroy, who hung around him and stuck to him like a big solid shadow.

I liked Moroy. I was fascinated by the way he talked and the way he thought. He had a kind of thinking you could trace with a firm straight line. He was wide and solidly built, moonfaced and foul-mouthed, with squinted, slanted eyes and crooked teeth. He liked to kid with me, turning his big body with startling quickness, reaching out with a fat hand to throw a fake jab or flick an ear.

69

MOROY'S TRADEMARK WAS A SMALL SHALLOW CRATER ON THE BACK of his neck, the size and shape of an old ten-centavo coin and colored a dark, violent purple. I was sure it was from a bullet. Whenever I asked him about it he would promise me that one day he would tell me all that I needed to know.

It made sense to hire someone who knew what it felt like to take a bullet. But even then I knew it was foolish to have a bodyguard who was also your driver. Still, My father insisted on having Moroy around as minder, chauffeur, errand-boy and right-hand man. Moroy did enjoy driving our 1976 Mr. Slim, solid, swift and perfect from its three-point chrome star, to its extended rear bumper. The engine started with a deep shudder, as though it were shrugging off sleep, and its heavy, bulletproof body moved with a low roar.

Moroy told me about my father's hidden life, his secret schedule. Sometimes he would need Moroy to drive him to the airport for the next flight to Hong Kong or Jakarta for an overnight trip. Or he would be at a five-star hotel, drinking and talking with businessmen and ambassadors. Or the Floating Casino, coming out in the morning hours wearing that same poker face.

Whenever he had to go somewhere my father would call for Moroy from the garage. He would pick up my presence, perched in my mango tree, in the corner of his vision, and send me scurrying into his room to retrieve his clutchbag. I remember it, black, heavier than it looked, with an evasive smell that dared me to open it while he wasn't watching. It held papers, checkbooks, thick bundles of dollar bills and a gun.

My father wanted me to become a lawyer like him. He spoke to me about how much trouble he had gone through for me. I knew the way to make a kid serious was to warn him about the consequences. He told me if I didn't study I'd end up like Moroy, whose meager future depended solely on his master, and whose job, ultimately, was to be expendable.

Moroy handed his gun to me once. There was so much to touch, so much to feel. There were ridges, incisions, screwheads, crisscross patterns, pinholes, nipples. It smelled of oil and metal. My hand could not refuse its shape and held it the only way it allowed, tightly embraced around the grip, pointer finger slipping into the trigger's hollow. I went further and aimed it at the sky and pulled the trigger; he had second-guessed me and it was empty, but the force felt so real. Something clicked and the gun vibrated with a tight metallic sound that startled even Nilda, who just glared at us. "One day," Moroy whispered, "you'll shoot a loaded gun, with real bullets."

Nilda's duty was to pay attention to me, to take notice of me, every inch, ever part, every blemish and scar, from the sunbaked hair she shampooed every day to the toenails she clipped every three weeks. She was fresh from the province, pale and very young, hired by my mother to replace the old woman who had been wet nurse, maid and servant for several years.

I spent the length of the summer climbing the mango trees at the edge of our front yard. They were tall and thick enough to spread over our concrete fence, and gave our house a dark, imposing presence.

But from my low branch, the light was gentle and I found I could feel the breezes that glanced off our small swimming pool in the middle of the terrace. As the day advanced I saw the tree's shadow grow longer on the grass and the dogs bark in relief, before everything quieted down toward evening.

At dinnertime my father had Nilda fetch me from the tree, and I opened my arms to let the afternoon's bounty tumble into her outstretched skirt. In the twilight her legs looked very white, against the mango tree's dark bark and my own skinny brown legs.

Nilda had come from a province overgrown with mango trees. She taught me how to climb our tree and pick its fruit. She taught me how to peel them and how to eat them. She taught me how to make the three sauces that made three different flavors. It was Nilda who tasted of the green mango we ate, both of us sitting by the pool in the sun and the heat. It was her tongue in my mouth during that long kiss. On that first hot day by the pool, she opened herself to me and her thighs held on to my small body. The sun beat on my head like a hammer, and as I grew hard I felt a headrush, as though the impossible length and girth of my manhood had dissipated me. I had thought it would make me stronger, but here, nothing was predictable. The rush came, from nowhere and from everywhere. She was silent as she held me and only whispered, yes, as she guided me into her, dark and wet, smelling of the sun and the pool chlorine, like nothing else I had ever seen or felt.

At first I couldn't move. I felt my knees gripped in a rubbery tension. I put a dozen images in my head. Moroy had demonstrated this movement to me by pumping a dirty finger in a tightly rolled fist. "One day you'll do this!" he had told me, and when I stuck my own finger in my fist he laughed because I didn't get it. But once from my tree I saw two dogs turning around each other in what I had thought was a heat-crazed stupor as they struck and mounted, joints frozen as the male pumped into the female.

72

But Nilda felt like no fist. And instead of holding still and waiting, she moved with me and around me. Moroy promised me I would feel like a man after my first time, but I felt I had been swallowed whole, a small boy with salty, sweating skin sliding into her opening.

Over lulls in my father's schedule, Moroy took me exploring. We ventured through tight roads, into tough neighborhoods. I marvelled at the the dark, cramped houses, the streetcorners and the sidewalks packed with people, places I never knew could exist. Moroy was a policeman once, and this had been his beat. He knew people wherever we went, the security guards at warehouse gates, the bums that hung out in front of gambling dens and sari-sari stores, the tough guys guarding the beer garden doors. When we walked those streets he squared his shoulders and walked a little slower than usual. It was like a killer's walk. He enjoyed the moment, savoring every step, while I tried to match his stride.

By his silence and the slightly changed expression on his face I always knew when my father was worried about something. I knew enough about the times to understand that things were changing.

Later that week my father went out into the yard, in his pajamas, in the middle of the night, and fired his gun into the sky. Through my window and saw his thin, hunched form snapping back with every shot. It looked like his body would break apart. The muzzle flash burst like tails of comets crashing into earth. I ran into his room and saw my mother crying, her face in her pillow. The clutchbag lay on his bedside table. The shots deafened me and I could hear nothing in the quick, silent spaces between. Then there was a long pause before it started again. Nilda came up behind me and pulled me back into my room, holding me tight and talking to me. She was used to this, she told me. In her town they had domestic disputes, police rubouts, exchanges between the military and the NPA. They would sit quietly and wait it out, wondering who'd been killed. In the morning the news would come around, a vice-mayor or a barangay captain dead, or a group of soldiers, or ordinary townfolk.

My father must have used up four or five magazines that night. I tried not to think of the possibility of the bullets returning to earth. Every Christmas season we heard stories about bullets being fired into the air and lodging themselves into young boys' skulls in their downward trajectory. We all pretended everything was normal when he appeared in the kitchen the next morning, in his thin, dark suit, cradling his clutchbag. He fixed Moroy with a hard look and told him to prepare for a long drive.

School starts when summer ends. After my first day, Moroy picked me up at the gate with energetic honks. He greeted me with a grin, like there was something he couldn't wait to tell me. He drove slow, letting the engine's slow churn fill the silence. Outside the sun had begun to turn a darker yellow.

We drove out the high school road, past the football fields. Outside my window the buildings slipped by, the gym, the chapel and the grade school. He turned into the side road that led to the seminary. He was still grinning, tapping his thumbs on the wheel. His grin was sinister, like he was planning to do something clever and terrible. The blood flowed from my arms and legs and I imagined he could bash my head in and bury me under the bushes without anyone ever knowing.

He stopped the car, pulled up the handbrake, opened the door and stepped out. He came over to my side and gestured to the driver's seat and the wheel. I scooted over and gave the gas a few hard pumps. On the dashboard the needle rose past the red mark as the buzz of the engine drilled into my back. I drove the clutch to the floor with my left foot and released it slowly, allowing the balance of my strength to creep into my right. I negotiated a three-point turn and headed out into the main campus troad. Moroy reached over to the back seat and retrieved his gun, placing it on the dashboard with a thud.

We passed college students walking to their classes. If they looked closely they would have seen the gun, blueblack and tinted orange from the late afternoon sun. Moroy pointed to a side road that opened into a hidden clearing, covered by an undisturbed layer of dead leaves. I stopped the car and shut off the engine. When I opened the door, the sounds of the school had gone. Moroy took the gun, unloaded it, and jammed a fresh magazine into the grip, producing small, startling sounds, a click, a low sliding screech, a louder click. Then he drew the slide back and let it spring forward with a final snap. He handed the gun to me and I held it with both hands, close to the center of my body. I could feel it against my groin. In my lap it sucked up the lines and folds of cloth into its metal center.

We stopped out onto the leaves and the grass. He motioned me over to the edge of the clearing, where the trees began. I held the gun low, thinking of where it was pointed.

"OK stop," he said. We had gone some distance into the trees, where the only things I could hear were our own movements disturbing the fallen leaves and the brown undergrowth.

"Now aim it at that tree and shoot." Moroy had picked a tree at random.

I raised the gun, looking at my hands like they weren't my own. He gripped my hands and taught me to hold it with my right hand taking aim and squeezing the trigger, my left hand cupped like a cradle to keep steady and cushion the recoil. My arms trembled with the great weight.

"Now shoot."

Something in me refused. Maybe it was the image of my father shooting into the empty air, his thin frame absorbing the blow.

"What's the matter with you? Squeeze the trigger!"

Nothing happened. Moroy's moonface broke into a fat smile. "I know about you and Nilda," he said.

I fired fast and blind, imagining myself emptying the clip into Moroy's big skull. The smoke that followed each explosion quickly cleared, but the smell of gunpowder remained, along with a kind of nerve shock.

Moroy smiled and put his hand on my shoulder. It was his way of telling me everything was alright, my secret was safe with him. We walked to the tree so I could look at the exploded bark and the clean round holes in the white wood underneath. Out of the corner of my eye I could see Moroy looking at me. When he moved toward me I swung around and kept him in sight. He flashed his signature smile, took the gun and congratulated me on a job well done.

We returned to the school parking lot, where Moroy asked me to treat him to fishballs and Coke.

Moroy prided himself on once being the mayor's "trigger." But when his boss lost the next election there was only his old police detachment to return to. Then he started working freelance for government officials and big businessmen.

I asked Moroy about the kind of trouble my father was having. Things were changing, he told me. He was even in danger of losing his job.

"Where would you go?" I teased him. "He made me you too comfortable. Now look at you. You're fat and spoiled."

He smiled and turned to me, hunched his shoulders, bobbed his big head and threw slo-mo jabs at the air. Then he sat down and gave a thoughtful smile. He looked down at his shoes and I saw the ten-centavo scar. "And you're slow," I added.

That night, Nilda held me locked into her by twisting her legs around mine. I felt unnatural. I couldn't stop. I came, my body jerking uncontrollably. It must have looked funny, my small body plugged into hers, my eyes rolled up inside their sockets, my lips curled and trembling. It took all the energy from me. Minutes later, she turned to me with a fresh look of hunger and excitement in her eyes and asked me if I wanted another one.

While Nilda and I spent the long, rainy after-school hours together, my father's secret trips with Moroy grew more frequent. One night in September, on one of those trips, a van sidled up to the SEL as it sped along the coastal road. The windows opened, guns poked out and opened fire. A brief chase followed, then the inevitable crash. The scene was littered with blood, glass shards and spent shells. They even showed it on TV. Policemen and reporters crowded over the wrecked car.

That was the one encounter Moroy didn't survive. He was too slow and too fat, and besides, he was driving. As the van gained on them, Moroy swung the car from side to side. When the van sped ahead and spun to block their way he tried to sweep it to the side. When the twisted metal of the van locked with the car's fender and did not let go he steered and drove the car's bulletproof bulk into it. Then he threw himself to the backseat to cover my father's body with his own. Five or six men stumbled out of the van. They fired pointblank at the SEL's windshield until the bulletproof glass gave way and then poked their guns through the holes. But the bullets couldn't poke through Moroy. The TV cameras showed him lying with his arms outstretched, spreading his body out. Moroy's hand still gripped his gun, still unfired. He had that same grin frozen on his moonface. He seemed pleased with his irrefutable logic.

The few bullets that had found their way around Moroy's body punched through my father's legs and narrowly missed his windpipe. The emergency doctors at Makati Med thought he was dead on arrival, but eventually discovered a weak pulse. Hours later he was lucid enough to recount the ambush in vivid detail. At Moroy's funeral the mayor came and spoke gravely about how this bodyguard had once taken a bullet for him, too.

Months later, my father could walk again, only with a very stiff limp. He looked like a hollowed-out tree. He had taken a long vacation and spent most of his time at home. He had a nurse who pushed him around the house in a wheelchair. He spoke with a raspy, exhausted voice, but told me how he still wished me to become a lawyer.

He bought me a second-hand car for my graduation. It rattled and the airconditioner sometimes didn't work. The week before school, Nilda and I rode the Marcos highway fast and hard, all the way to Fairview, where there was a huge empty mall where nobody went but they still played movies, even to empty theaters. We bought ice cream and we watched a Tagalog movie. Five minutes into it she leaned against me, took my hand and brought it up her skirt, between her thighs. It felt warm and very tender to be touching her there. It felt as though what had happened between us was ages before.

Nilda left at the end of the month. Yayas become redundant when their wards are grown. I was fourteen, entering high school at the end of the summer. My mother gave her a ticket for the boat ride home, along with a month's pay.

Nilda's eyes were red and wet with tears while she undressed me, slipped her uniform off and joined me for our last bath together. I planted my feet on hers and kissed the hollow of her shoulder. It felt good to know her body. I knew where she liked to be touched and kissed, and how her many different parts tasted. I pressed myself against her, covering her body with mine, from the skin on my face to the soles of my feet.

Nilda laid out her bags and her boxes in the living room and opened them in front of my mother for inspection. I saw her uniforms, her bathing suit and her pink underwear and noticed that she had snuck in two of my old sport shirts, folded tight and small. There was also a photo of me as a boy, in an old silver frame. My mother wordlessly put it back on the piano where it belonged, beside pictures of my father.

I put her bags in the back of the car and we drove in silence to the port area. On the way I asked her what she was planning to do back home. She said she didn't know. She turned to me and said she wanted to stay with me and go with me wherever I wanted to go. "Uban ko nimo," she said, in the language she had taught me, what they spoke at home. I threw her a smile and offered to visit her one day. She laughed bitterly and asked me if I even remembered where she lived. Of course, I said, where there were mango trees all over. •

Self with dog, 1997

JORGE LANDICHO HESITATES AT THE DOOR. IT IS HIS FIRST VISIT TO the art dealer's flat, and already he feels strange, in a place so calm and quietly removed, twenty-four floors up. He wonders to himself why he never thought about living in a condominium. At home his dog has the run of his small yard. He picks up scents and barks even before visitors knock, his paws make sounds like sparks across the pavement, and growling low, he pounces on the gate with his full weight and muscle.

Jorge bends toward the door, trying to pick up any noise, and is startled by a shadow behind the eyehole. The door opens and behind it is James Fojas, a man whose age is difficult to guess. He is wearing wire-rimmed glasses and behind them his eyes are quick and bright.

The flat is wide and white. From the door there is a short hallway that, on its left, opens into a large, open room. The wall on the right is covered with paintings, the chaos interrupted only by three white doors. When James shows him in he sees that the large room is lit with a natural brightness, opening through French doors into a wide balcony.

It is morning and the skies are light brown and the light from the balcony is hard and crystalline. James points out that such bright light, only slightly polarized by the cloud cover and the tropical atmosphere, is perfect for viewing paintings. Jorge's indoctrination begins with a tour of his collection, which, James apologetically adds, is a mishmash, a montage, a crude pile.

There are small pieces by the young and unknown, in unframed canvases, on board, and on freshly unrolled paper. There are enormous flowers, ripe and unripe fruit, young boys playing in rivers. There are monkey-eating eagles, fighting dogs and nudes in various settings and poses. James points out the differences between glossy acrylic, gentle watercolor and dark, complex oil.

Then James shows him the cream, hanging high on the wall in identical frames. In a pieta by Kiukok the man is a bent, desperate skeleton, and the woman, muscled and defiant, both figures joined in colors of flesh, earth and hardened blood. In a sketch by Ocampo, three spare lines are all it takes to fill the flesh-colored space, blurring into a woman's shape, form and skin. A Manansala nude is made full and slow-moving by strokes of thick black charcoal.

Jorge randomly picks a painting from those leaning against the wall—an oil-on-wood of a fish vendor signed "Ballardo 1980." Out of curiosity, he asks James how much he wants for it.

James clears his throat and murmurs the first of many lessons in his ear: that sometimes color can be a shape and shape can be a color. That in the hands of someone truly gifted, line, color, shape, frame, all are interconnected and interchangeable. Soon, lines are bent, color is removed from color, shape is shrugged off, the frame disappears and meaning appears. No longer do we see coherent structure, individual characters, but powerful themes, spiritual movement.

81

Suddenly, we feel the impulses we cannot experience, the passion we can't afford to have. "And that, my friend, makes a really good painting almost priceless."

JAMES INVITES JORGE TO AN EXHIBIT OPENING. JORGE GETS THERE early, but the party is already in full swing. He finds James by the bar, in a red shirt, leather pants and a cowboy hat, talking to a young girl with green hair and a nose ring. Jorge is in his mall clothes. He doesn't recognize the painter, by work or by name. There are fifteen of his works, large and complicated, in mixed media, spread out along one side of the gallery.

They take the tour and Jorge stops before a Madonna and Child, done in cut-up newspaper and stained in shades of red and sepia.

Under James' guidance Jorge studiously marks the golden mean, seeks out the source of light, follows the path of the eye. The lines of the mother's arm and jaw lead him to a sun that hangs low and dim over her shoulder, where the child perches, small and faceless.

James cocks his hat and smiles at Jorge. "I have some of his old stuff. You'll find them to be better than any of these. Don't be foolish enough to fall for the gallery price."

BRUNO IS A ROTTWEILER IN BLACK AND DULL BROWN, FOUR-FOOT high at the shoulder. He consumes a sack of chow in two weeks. He is beautiful and expensive, a concession to the rising crime rate. When Jorge comes home Bruno growls and rattles on the gate with his weight, but is quick, heavy and lavish with instinctive affection.

SELF WITH DOG, 1997

Jorge Landicho lives in a townhouse off Tomas Morato Avenue and manages the money his parents left him two years ago. He is heavily into stocks—oils, second stringers, some blue chips. His modest inheritance, along with the current swell of interest in equity investments, give him the freedom to remain unemployed and unencumbered by routine, molded expectation, and the prefabrications and trappings of career and ambition.

He sees his father's death as a renaissance. He sees himself to be part of that young generation, overqualified and under forty, with the rare ability to make markets move and form lush mountains out of the rocky business landscape.

Jorge puts rice in the cooker and dumps a packet of instant noodles in simmering water. He rips open a fresh sack of dog food, pouring the meaty chunks into one shallow bowl and filling another with fresh water. For himself he retrieves a pot of adobo from the refrigerator and sets it on the stove. He sprinkles water on a plate of rice and puts the plate in the microwave.

83

The light from outside is fading fast. As Bruno grunts and slobbers over his bowl, Jorge looks intently, earnestly at his lot, hanging on his living room walls. The paintings refract and swell under the color, and inside him he feels something swirling, rising like the tide.

This is how he felt when he saw his first Amorsolo, his first Luna, his first Hidalgo. He was in Malacañang Palace on a group tour. They had a great collection of large canvases, but eroded by seasons of dust and years of neglect, oblivious to the routine rounds of the security guards and common clerks. The tour guide made the dramatic suggestion that these were once overshadowed by even greater works, lost over the years to presidential plunder.

Jorge looks at the opacity of fruits, the thick strokes of sunsets and landscapes glowing in the afternoon light. But his living room is peopled most of all by faces, in smudged oil, in silky gouache, in silver pencil, with eyes everywhere looking at him as he sits in his chair and crosses his legs.

The business news is on. Jorge remembers the Madonna and Child and imagines it hanging in his home, a mosaic of headlines frozen in red: murder, rape and scandal among the sports scores, weather forecasts and financial warnings about the stock market finally reaching the inevitable downside of its cycle.

With each hesitation Jorge forgoes, with each check he writes, the floors and the walls of James Fojas' apartment shrink a little more and he feels bigger, stronger. What seemed to be a white space filled with squares of mysterious shape and color has become, in a matter of months, a tiny flat, laid out like a cramped, almost oppressive inverted letter L, closed in by layers of canvases new and long unsold, like rows of prodigious, multicolored teeth. Jorge looks around and sees birdcages, cockfights, cathedrals, vortices of color, vague shapes and mottled forms that recall to him old terrors and childhood images.

James shows him a Florian of a young couple, naked, their flesh tinted fluorescent blue. 1962, 24 x 36. The man is covered by the woman's embrace, and looks at Jorge Landicho with the knowing, indifferent gaze of immortal boredom. Or perhaps, he thinks, it is the half-lidded look of the lust-consumed. The pose is sexual, but their features asexual. The bodies are pressed together, not for warmth, perhaps, but in anatomical prayer, or in a cold, otherworldly affinity.

"It's called 'Young Venus,' Jorge, and I can tell you, oh boy, that this is something totally different. The folks at

84

Singapore went nuts over this. But you know, honestly, I couldn't bear to see it leave this country. For whatever it's worth, I still have that feeling sometimes, you know? Did you know that I was an activist when I was younger? But this is different, I tell you. This time I really mean what I say when I say this is different. Somebody hid this beauty under a fucking rock, in a fucking cave, and I was lucky enough to have the key."

"Done very well," James adds. "Reminds me of early Francis Bacon. Now that was a mathematician." Jorge smiles, nods, and squints. James retrieves a book from a shelf and shows him page after page of Francis Bacon. He points out the measured planes, the intersecting lines, the flesh folded and pressed into grotesque shapes.

The antique table in the middle of James' apartment is a table for negotiations, discussions and dinner. James is quick to point out the inescapable logic of using the same substrate for business, pleasure and reward.

"Sit here so you can see it better." Jorge sits with his back to the balcony light, facing the artwork. He sits across the table in front of him.

His eyes remove themselves from "Young Venus," travel across the wall, and settle on another vortex, the dark navel of a reclining nude, her face concealed by a mask in the form of an owl's face, with blank round eyes and a hooked beak, crowned with feathers of green and yellow ochre.

James quickly follows his eyes. "Munying Maskiar's 'Masked Odalisque,'" he whispers. "It's where all men's eyeballs drown. You will see that Munying has made a paradox of her. She is naked, but her face will never be known. It's a seduction. But a seduction without emotion, without the human face. She seduces us only with shape and with color."

Jorge shifts his gaze to the owl-like features. "Behind the mask, she knows you want her. But she wants you, too, and tells you so, with the way she arranges her arms, her hips, her legs, her very navel. All without giving you the pleasure of her eyes or her expression."

Jorge Landicho looks away and affords himself a secret grimace at James' sales talk. Still, he feels himself drawn to her outstretched arm, the sharp, flesh-colored border of her body, the face he will never see. The mask reminds him of ostrich feathers, incense sticks, Arabic writing. And in the shadows behind her, he imagines other women, bound in the oily darkness.

To restore his calm Jorge reminds himself that he is speaking to a middleman, a mercenary, someone who can easily read quick excitement and naïve contemplation, and convert such muddled feelings into passion, even obsession. Jorge looks at his watch and recognizes a comfortable hour, long after the mesmerizing heat of noon and the urgency of approaching dinnertime.

Jorge goes to the balcony and sees the green of the golf course beneath him. He sees the strings of kites snarled on the electric lines. It's January again. The year promises to be small and nondescript, with nothing but more news of failing markets and a tired government in the middle of its term.

He returns to his chair, sits back, swings a leg and bides his time.

"You're absolutely right," James says, voice grave and low. "You're being smart about it. This piece is not for the impulsive. It's not for the brute. It's for the patient. It's for the intelligent. The meanings creep in strong and slow. Only the most uncivilized rely on gut feel. Take your time, Jorge. It sure did. It took more than thirty years to show itself to you, but it

86

might have been painted yesterday, visualized today, imagined and dreamt of tomorrow. It fools time and it fools the mind."

Jorge suddenly hears random sounds form behind the wall of canvases: dull footsteps, a television switching channels, the churn of airconditioning, the twist of the tap and the rustle of water.

He glances at James, and there are no signs he is married. He never thought to ask. Though he is possibly in his middle forties, and he has lines on his forehead and a grey fringe of hair near his temples, he wears no ring. He looks quiet and relaxed, dressed this afternoon in a yellow plaid shirt, stiff jeans and expensive-looking leather sandals. His hobbies betray the carefree, extravagant joys of the affluent and unattached: he spoke once of a diving trip with friends, on another time an evening at the Casino, or a particularly energetic and relaxing session at the massage parlor, or, more recently, watching visiting amateur Russian ballerinas at the Cultural Center.

He remembers him speaking once of women. That was over port and cigars in celebration of Jorge's purchase of a 4 by 8-foot oil on board by Hermes Alonzo. It took a month of needling and haggling, and ended triumphantly for both sides. Jorge confessed it took a huge chunk out of his savings, and James revealed to Jorge how sad he was to let the Alonzo go, because the artist did not make such ambitious pieces anymore. The purchase finally deserved him a heart-to-heart talk, a personal account of one of James' extraordinary pursuits. This one was of a well-known actress whom the dealer had kept in a hotel suite for a month, living on nothing but drugs, food and sex. Those were in his younger days, when he was still painting. He could sell out three consecutive one-man shows in six months and drove a top-down Benz. He performed stills, social commentaries, portraits. He painted everyone, even the president, who summoned him to do a mural of the first family—his biggest, and last, work. In '87 he went surreal and had a nervous breakdown.

Behind James, one of the white doors opens, for the first time in all of Jorge Landicho's visits. A young girl appears. She is in a sport shirt and jeans and carries a small wooden tray with coffee cups and a plate of biscuits. The softness of her form draws in the afternoon light, and her hair, wet from a bath, gathers a liquid yellow glow.

James states a ridiculous, multisyllabic price. Before Jorge can say anything he brings it down, by a margin that is meant to be proportional to the magnitude of their friendship, first as friends of friends, and now as cultivated, accomplished, attuned lovers of fine art.

"I don't think I've introduced you to my daughter, Margarita" the dealer says.

Margarita gives Jorge a brief look, and sets the tray on the table.

Jorge feigns fullness, fighting the urge to append his mild protestation with a rub of the tummy.

"She takes tennis lessons—"

James blinks behind his glasses as Jorge Landicho interrupts to produce a checkbook. He scrawls an amount, signs the check and tears it out.

"Bring out some sherry," he says to Margarita. "Why don't you have dinner here, Jorge. My daughter's only nineteen but she can cook anything mean and quick. What kind of food do you like?"

"I'm going out tonight, Dad," Margarita announces.

"Never mind. We'll go out to eat," the dealer says.

"Don't worry about me," Jorge says, managing a quick look at his watch. "I have a dinner appointment."

As usual, the dealer arranges for a time to make the delivery of the painting and the certificate of provenance at Jorge's home. He shows him to the door, making a last offer for dinner. Margarita comes out of the bedroom, smelling of perfume. She is carrying a duffel bag and a tennis racket. She nods to her father and walks out, past the men, to the elevator bay.

Jorge Landicho emerges into the driveway, where the night is warm and all is quiet, save for the soft, muffled sounds of the street beyond the hedges that surround the condominium. Margarita is there, waiting on the pavement, a tall figure in jeans and a sport shirt, looking out toward the empty street.

She glances at Jorge and offers a vague look of recognition.

Jorge trembles, blinks, thinks to act suave, utters his name in a reflex formed out of cocktail parties and conventions. He offers a hand to shake, and recalls his first meeting with his art dealer, her father. He remembers the story and wonders if Margarita's mother was that actress, that woman who was, he recalls, so beautiful on television and in the movies.

Margarita smiles shyly, a curve of light appearing on her cheek, then swiftly disappearing as she turns toward the sound of a car crunching gravel and going up the driveway. She opens the passenger door, swings her duffel bag and tennis racket inside, enters the car, and pulls the door shut. In the darkness of the driver's side Jorge sees the shape of a man's face, lit faintly by the glow of a cigarette. He watches as she takes the cigarette from him and sticks it in her mouth. He imagines that he sees her face a split second before it turns, looking at him with an expression that hides, in its infinite colors, shades of helplessness, sadness, pity and utter disdain.

SELF WITH DOG, 1997

Jorge Landicho returns home to a hungry dog and the smell of stale food and unwashed plates in the kitchen. He turns on the living room lights and imagines where his new painting might be, replacing perhaps the Ballardo fish vendor, which to him has always seemed too folksy, too ordinary, or the perhaps the Ambrosio portrait, now too light and flat. The Ambrosio was the first major piece he purchased, not off his dealer but from the artist himself. James brought him along to the studio. There was an unfinished canvas on the easel, a background in dark and complex layers, upon which the artist had penciled vague figures. "Are you selling this?" he asked the artist, then pressured him for a friendly price, as James himself had taught him.

In this manner, he sees his collection taking shape, through the long and difficult months, beginning from a bright moment of inspiration, then a period of darkness, of a muddled confusion, before finally coming through. He sits in his living room, mesmerized and nauseated by the colors and the faint smell of rotting food.

In the morning, the phone rings while Jorge is in the middle of preparing the dog's meal. Bruno hasn't been fed all day.

He is unfamiliar with the voice on the other end. "Mr. Landicho, you wrote out a check last week?" Yes, I remember the date, Jorge answers, seeing Margarita holding a tray full of porcelain in the slant of the afternoon sun. I even remember the time. He remembers writing out the check, laughing privately at the amount and wondering how he would cover it. He remembers calling his broker to unload the last batch of blue chips. PLDT, Metrobank, I don't care, what's the difference, sell the lot.

The march of events, a series of patterns, broken images and reflections swiftly gathers order. Yes, I know the date I wrote on the check. No. Was it the other week? The other day?

He remembers the bar of light across her cheek, the sound of her voice, so different from this woman talking to him, correcting him: the check was dated yesterday and clears today, and unfortunately, you have no funds to cover it.

Bruno growls. He is a black and brown blur in slow motion as he scampers toward the door, a split second before Jorge hears the knocking on the gate outside. He tells the woman to hold, stands up and scans his living room. In the afternoon light the paintings look rich and heavy, their clumps of hardened paint like clotted soup. He looks out through the blinds and sees black leather sandals under the gate, the bottom part of a wooden frame resting on them.

91

Outside, the sunlight is bright and prismatic. Jorge notices for the first time the flaking layer of green paint on the metal gate, the metal latch catching a spectrum of color from the morning sun. He feels the white flare on his scalp and nape as he grips Bruno by the collar, feeling a slow, deep growl build in his body as he gathers strength for an attack.

Now, as the knocking continues, "Masked Odalisque" takes precedence over his vision. The woman with an owl's face, her flesh cast in dark light: a picture of love and desire. He remembers it as though it were a wild night of passion, a vivid scene from an old movie, or an unforgettable meal. Jorge realizes he can recall it stroke for stroke, color for color, this painting, along with all the other images in his gallery, even without needing to see any of them, the faces, the bodies and the places, coming in cruel and tender in the middle of the morning. •

Ghosts

LYNN SMELLED IT IN THE MIDMORNINGS, CREEPING UP FROM MAYBE two balconies down, coming through the laundry room window, into the dining room, across well-scrubbed tiles, where it picked a path among the colors on the carpeting, the scents of dinner, of last night's whiskey and wine, up her calves, slipping into the easy grooves of her house dress, hanging in the still, bright air and drifting into her nose, from where she imagined it wound its way down into her stomach, through her blood, and into her womb, where her baby, three weeks old, smelled it and perhaps recognized it, too: the durian, king of fruits, large, thorny outside and yellow and thick like spoiled milk inside. "Tastes like heaven, smells like hell," the foreigners quipped. She could eat a mountain of it when she was a child. Now she had had enough of the fruit and the old joke, but she could not stop the smell.

Her amos had entertained guests until late the night before, but as always, were up by seven and had a cab waiting for them at eight-thirty. Lynn had remained asleep through all this and didn't rise till nine, to a table with last night's dinner settings and a day's worth of chores laid out for her. Any of her previous employers might have scolded her for being tardy, but she felt lucky enough to have a kababayan couple as her amos, who afforded her more than a small measure of kindness.

The durian was opened like clockwork—when the smell hit the air she knew it was ten-thirty. Even so, Lynn treasured hours like these when the apartment was all hers. She would turn up the TV in their room, taking care to remember the channel and volume settings. Sometimes she would power up their hi-fi system. They had warned her not to touch it, because the components were expensive and very delicate, especially the vacuum tube amplifiers that ran hot—so she turned them on in the exact sequence she had seen Kuya Noel do it. In idle afternoons she played her CDs and danced the "otso-otso" the way she had seen it in her friends' videotapes.

There was this space, between the morning rush and the noontime chores, and there was the afternoon stretch after everything had been done and she was only waiting for one of them to arrive—usually Ate Lara, who called ahead to inform her whether they would be eating out that night or she would be preparing dinner herself. This was a good early warning device.

There was also the quiet hour after they retired to their bedroom and she had finished tidying up the kitchen. She punctuated that private time with a twist of the clothesdryer dial: the timer ticked and the red light came on, and she groped the top of the laundry shelf for her cigarettes and smoked two or three on the small balcony by her quarters, before curling up to sleep with a Tagalog romance novel.

Sometimes, from out on the balcony, she heard her amos making love, the sound of their happy sighs tripping quietly through the dry Singapore air. They had been trying for a baby, Ate Lara had confessed to her once. It was the only

93

thing that was missing. They'd been here two years already, and were already quite adjusted to life in the new city. They had found good friends among the expatriate community, bankers and managers, Pinoys like themselves, who they shared weekends with. Sometimes they drove to East Coast Park, where the beach reminded them of the Mindoro surf and whose divespots almost recalled the deep off the Batangas coastline.

Lynn remembered her own seaside, where she went with her mother when she was very young. The busride took them outside their town and led them further outward, to the southern coast. Ma-a beach was a deserted sweep of rough beige sand. It hurt the feet when she walked barefoot across it but there was also a pleasure she couldn't resist. Years later she remembered it when she made love for the first time, to Tiboy, a kind of pain that was gentle and firm, that moved when she moved and stopped when she stopped. She looked at her mother, and there she was, a stretch of beach, standing still and looking at her.

The day that she remembered at Ma-a beach was her birthday, and in the morning of that day she grimaced as her mother marked her forehead with a bright red cross of chicken blood. Blood attracted good fortune and warded off the bad stuff. Her mother also told her not to walk on her knees unless she was in church, because it made you see ghosts of old relatives. I knew she meant the ghost of her mother, the one they called Lola Glo, fat and fearsome-looking, with piercing eyes and stringy white hair—which was how she looked even when she was alive.

On Saturdays Lolo Angel would take her along in the twincab for a ride out of Mabini and into the city. Her mother would frown at him for spoiling her, but he never listened to her when it came to his granddaughter. The twincab bore his name, painted on the sides, below "Emergency Rescue" and above "Barangay Captain." There was also "Official Use Only,'" stencille in red, right above the rear wheel. "Official use also," Lolo would laughingly say to their mother. To Lynn, it was her first official transport out of the fields and dirt roads.

Tagum City was the first city in her life. It was hot, dark, and dusty. Her lolo took her to the arcades and the shopping centers and the markets, all cloudy with dust and cigarette smoke. The air was always full of the sound of jeepneys and their diesel scent. When Lynn returned her mother was always waiting with a good meal. Lynn and her grandfather knew it was her way of saying not everything came from the city, that their town was good for something, too. During the afternoon they were away she had had the house cleaned and their things tidied: the books and magazines were back on theis shelves and Lynn's toys back in their baskets, returned carefully to their place above the aparador that dominated the small upstairs living room.

After a long bath and before retiring to bed, mother and daughter always brushed their long hair with a hundred slow strokes. They looked in the mirror and remarked with wide smiles how little difference there was between them—perhaps in Lynn's eyes, slightly turned down at the corners, or there in her mother's cheek, identically spare and smooth, save for a dimple, her mother teased, tracing its almost invisible edge with a finger. When Lynn turned to show it to the mirror the dimple disappeared and they remained, for the time being, identical twins.

For boys their town had few. It was only during her high school years that her interest was ignited by a dark-skinned transferee from the city, Tiboy—short for City Boy—who

95

wore his nickname proudly. He was beautiful, even when Lynn knew the truth about him: he had been recalled back to the province, ruefully, by his parents, because he had begun to slack off in school and started going with the wrong crowd and was even, some whispered, suspected of being a drug addict. Back then nobody had ever met a real live addict before.

Tiboy wore real Nike shoes, not the fake ones the other boys bought from the market. He smoked Marlboro Lights, not the cheaper Miller or Memphis, and spoke just like the city boys that Lynn always saw in the Tagum City malls. But Tiboy was homegrown, just like her. His father tended a small ube plot for an absentee landlord and his mother sometimes made maruya and biko to augment their income. When Tiboy was not sitting at the corner store smoking and cursing and drinking Pale Pilsen—what they mostly drank in the city, instead of tuba or gin or fizzy Gold Eagle Beer—they knew he was helping out on the farm.

In the easy times between harvests, Tiboy smoldered for her love. As she sat on the wooden bench outside the sari-sari store he laid smoke rings in the air and threw smoky spears through them. Her silence was golden. It gripped him in a kind of fever while he waited for her to say something. She was cruel to Tiboy but that was the fashion of her age, to treat the ones you wanted like you couldn't care less about them. Like many girls their age it was her style to be cruel to boys and conniving with the girls. Their weekly immersions in the city gave them the edge—they made sure to buy the newest hairbands and plastic bracelets. Once in a while Lolo Angel would buy her the cassette of their choice—always music she always heard on TV: theme songs from the evening soap operas, or the loud dance music from the afternoon variety shows.

Tiboy was insistent. He sent flowers through a farmhand or a neighbor. They were sniffed at, displayed for a day, sniffed at again, then thrown into the trash, card and all. But even then, Lynn knew she would one day like him.

THIS, TOO, WAS THE MODE OF HER NEW LOVE. HE WORKED AT THE shipping line daytime and squeezed in time for her over the weekends. He waited for her at streetcorners and cafes, sometimes for hours, while she shopped for shoes with her friends and gossipped in the parks.

Just like her city boy, he was dark and smelled sharply of sun—amoy araw—not like the others, amoy ewan, smelling not of natural things but of something else she couldn't quite place a finger on. Spices? Sweat? She thought she could stand it when she had smelled it the first time at the airports, to her then an intriguing smell, exotic, then exciting, quickening as they filed into the tube for her first flight out of Manila. Then, she thought, to calm herself down, it was merely from one city to another, with crowds, roads and potholes.

Her first foreign airport was Chang-I. It quickly became her favorite place. The largest airport in the world, the brochure said. She filled her handcarry with free maps, guide books, magazines and leaflets. Even, she remembered, the pink advisory against tuberculosis and FMD, remembering also the thought balloon in her head, similarly pink: why, not me.

Then years later the tuberculosis became so real, as real as those cops she saw once, in Chang-I as well, on one of her rare trips home. The airport police were so armed to the teeth they looked like soldiers. After 9/11, who wouldn't be paranoid? Now she learned never to say "why, not me, of

97

course—it could never happen to me." And so she was glad to see them, a gaggle of them trooping from somewhere undisclosed to somewhere mysterious, denying themselves the convenience of the walk-a-lators and the brisk comfort of the golf carts that sped officiously through the smelly crowd, waving the slow ones aside with their brisk horns and yellow lights. They were the first and last Singapore policemen she ever saw, marching with a padded cadence, an Asian cadence, she had thought then, brisk and light, accommodating shorter legs and, perhaps, quicker minds. This was Chang-I airport but there was a Chang-I prison, too, it had dawned on her then, as much of the OFW-oriented literature had sought to remind her.

Tuberculosis, the word, turned as bright pink as the advisory paper, taking one of her closest friends and textmates by complete surprise, The woman had been working there all her life, leaving her marriage and her children behind but earning enough money to buy them a house and a Tamaraw FX—a kind of Toyota she'd never even seen, but, as her family had assured her, would be the workhorse for three businesses and last almost a lifetime. When the TB struck the image of the Chang-I cops returned.

Before the woman flew home there was a week of frantic calls for help. She was quarantined by her employers and given advice by the ministry. They tried to console her with text after text, and even pooled some cash together for her new life back home. It amounted to nothing much, but what could they do? A week later she called from Manila to tell her about how dark it was, how polluted, how they picked her up at the airport on the FX, battered from use and stuffed to overflowing with relatives, and she felt like turning around and going back.

The day it all became real to Lynn was a Sunday. She had awakened early, dressed carefully, deciding on a color combination she had never tried, put on some perfume, all to cheer herself up. She picked up the customary note left by her Ate Lara on the fridge, instructing her on what to prepare for dinner, slipped out the door, exited the apartment building and walked down the low hill to the bus station. She took the no. 5 bus and got off at the footbridge on Scott's Road, where there was a pharmacy at the other end.

In the subway restroom, she unloaded the plastic bag on the dresser. There was a pack of cigarettes and a pregnancy test kit. She lit a cigarette and read the label for contraindications. She unwrapped the white plastic stick and stood over the toilet bowl. She let go of her pee and poked the tip through the gentle stream. She smoked as she waited for the little window to show something.

99

A cleaning auntie was working in one of the toilet cubicles. She was old and small, and she thought of Aling Clara, who had left their town as a young woman. When she returned she had lost all her teeth and her body had bent so small that she was smaller than any of the twelve children she bore over all those years she was away. Unfair, she thought, remembering Lolo Angel at the same age—probably even older than this cleaning lady—still getting elected barangay captain and driving his twincab and drinking large amounts of gin. Men could grow old like that, sitting quietly and thinking about the lives they had lived while their wives and daughters kept them company, kept the house clean and laid the gin and the coffeepot on their table, with one glass and a cup and saucer.

There were times, for example, when she thought Lolo Angel only asked her to accompany her to the city because he needed someone to be with him, a minder, while he met with other government officials from other towns. It was this way too with some of her friends here. Their amos would invite them to a day of market-shopping or window-shopping—only because they needed someone to talk to during idle moments, or someone to eat with. It was a treat and it was a job, and you were lucky to have both.

While the leaflet that she carefully read clearly indicated through illustrations that she should expect—or not expect—an upright plus sign in the little white window, what developed was more like an X and not a plus, or at best it was a cross-eyed-plus. She held the plastic thing straight up, then straight across her vision. The X, crooked, unruly, gave her a strange comfort. That was probably why they called it the comfort room—the CR—as Filipinos called it, even when it was a lavatory such as in a plane or a washroom such as she once knew it in school. There was no single straight way to call it. From this angle it wasn't an X either. It was nullified, negative like a cocked die. It was haphazard, disorderly, like the way she marked her questionnaires—X single, married, separated, widowed. Tourist X overseas contract worker. Six months one year X other. Then the feeling was gone, those stupid thoughts flushed away, and she was all of a sudden sure and she was out of there, walking along Orchard Road again, slipping like any old permanent resident past the Filipinas and the Filipinos, Ngee Ann City Takashimaya and the vivid green corner at Scott's road. She knew she could walk blind and oblivious through all of Singapore and reach home without thinking a single thought, a U-Turn at the junction, up the hill, right at the apartment building, into the first elevator bay, out at the twentieth floor, left across the apartment where there lived an old Indian who owned a shopping mall. Everywhere here there were millionaires, if you counted up the dollars, added up the forced savings, took away the taxes and multiplied by

31 point something. Even that something was unimportant, taxes for the experience, spare change for the church at Zion Road, where, even as a newcomer, she knew they would be there, many of them who spoke Bisaya like her and who danced the "otso-otso" and knew who Kristine Hermosa was, with her big bust and her big white smile.

But X also meant cross-eyed and twisted, and would her baby be so? She had read somewhere that scientists could weed out defects from the mother's womb. Or had seen it from the Discovery Channel while she was dusting the master's bedroom. They were at the doorstep of a new world where the unborn and just conceived could be scanned and screened and decisions could be made that could never have been made before. Hair color, eye color, height and body type were determined like a multiple choice quiz: black brown X blonde, X blue brown black.

Lynn wondered where the unwanted would be received. There was a limbo for unbaptized babies. What might the limbo of the unwanted ones be? She thought of the multiple-choice quiz, like an election sheet she once saw when she went with a friend who wanted to cast a vote at the embassy, and laughingly lamented, as they munched on Mos Burgers at Plaza Singapura, how she had to choose among ex-teen idols and basketball players. Lynn imagined a country filled with cast-off choices, sent there to make a home out of what they had. Well, she thought, smiling a little, they would have each other.

Every six months they had to submit to a comprehensive medical exam. Pregnancy meant deportation. That was on a form somewhere, or a thought balloon perhaps, delivered to her by one of those instant friends she made at bible study sessions or while shopping. She made many friends that way.

It was the way she looked, maybe, somebody told her "maganda ang bukas ng mukha niya"—she had a face that opened beautifully, she tried to translate, into English first, then into Bisaya, though neither meant anything. The friend told her while they were being mischievous, "boy-watching" as they confessed to themselves, a guilty pleasure that counted among the archaic, like "joyriding," as Lolo Angel called it, into Tagum City.

The Filipinos looked like gods here, with their wavy black hair and deep, beautiful eyes. There was also that way of moving that breathed experience, in the long, slow flights and shiprides that took them through Athens, Paris, Abu Dhabi, London, Dublin and Dubai. They had families back home that waited for them, counted on their every word and every cent, and she guessed that was what made them look darker and shine brighter.

Like Tiboy, too, her new man promised her many things, and she knew that he was like a god that way, too—all full of promises and hope, but too burdened with responsibilities in this world and the other. That other world was home, or Ormoc, where he was trying to rebuild his family life, ravaged by that storm many years ago. It sounded like it was an excuse to avoid the responsibility but who knows, Lynn said, and remembered her own town and the first time she went home, many years ago.

"Let's just create a heaven on earth here," he had said. And he was serious when he said it. They'd done it right before and it was the time for guilt and seriousness. Lynn laughed at that. Remembering it now, she had the idea that she'd been laughing with his sperm fresh inside her, that by that time it had fertilized her egg: that was the baby's first laugh, at the baby's first joke. She knew, of course, that nothing would happen, that everything was semipermanent here.

But Lynn said yes, and even when she was late, maintained the idea that it might be heaven, to begin again. When she was young she was hooked on that. It was her grandfather, really, who would bring her whenever there was a new movie, a new store or restaurant. She could not believe then that a city could be always changing, that something could never be satisfied with its old self.

HER AMOS BROUGHT HOME A NEW TV THAT NIGHT. THEY MADE IT out like a surprise to Lynn because it meant she would be getting the old one for her room. They knew she longed to see the game shows and variety shows her friends would always talk about. They spent long Sunday afternoons watching tapes or talking about the latest celebrity gossip. Kuya Noel hooked up the cable and stepped back for her to see. His smile was proud—was it a little sweet and nervous?—while she testily flipped through a couple of channels. For a fleeting, fleeting moment she thought she could do it with him, be tender and firm with him, enough for him to like her, and there would be another moment, a blind one, in her room or in the laundry area or, for God's sake, as long as she was dreaming, in the master's bedroom. It would need only a moment, or even a moment within a moment. She could not deny that she had thought about it once or twice before, even as a stupid little momentary thought, but now, she knew that when things get desperate one thinks of the most desperate things.

As she stood on the dark balcony and looked at Kuya Noel's white underwear tumbling end over end in the window, he imagined life with him, and she could not deny that it would be a dream. For expats there were no restrictions at all. As she thought about their dinners out, their Sunday jaunts to the East Coast, her body was a tight, curled up shape under the bedsheets, trembling out of desperation, but in the presence of another being, like a ghost. Lolo's ghost, perhaps? She recalled the times before when she wished it would appear. But here it was, not a ghost, but her baby—her foetus, she corrected herself, remembering the Discovery Channel—another thing, an undefined presence, inside her, but outside her, too.

If she had a choice, she would make this a beautiful child a man, dark-skinned, certainly, with deep blue eyes—why not?—and a soft voice and wide, sharp shoulders upon which she could lay her head, tired of her whole life. He would be but eighteen or nineteen and she, old as her mother was and looking like her mother, too. Fifty-five, sixty, almost old enough to be his grandmother. Even married women and mothers would fall for him. 'Mariosep, even men would fall for him, because he would be gentle and refined and neutral.

She imagined him leaving him on the very last day of his youth, on the cusp of his birthday. High noon, the light full and hard on his features. "Aalis na ako 'Ma," Juan Pablo Miguel, as he would be christened—and why not? she always wanted a mestizo—would say, similarly leaving her, many years from now, an impossible sight with his dark hair and sinew, the jaw that looked especially strong and powerful from a certain angle, his knifelike look as he took the first jeep that trundled up the dusty road to the city. He would be gone anyway, 'no?—and it made no sense to think of him. But then, as she had always thought, as long as she was dreaming, there he was, a perfect child at the end of a long line, an impossible, imaginary character with an impossibly Spanish name.

She would leave him anyway, 'no? The way it was on the day she mentally shrugged off Angela and became simply: Lynn. She wanted to be serious, driven, no-nonsense. She knew three Angelas and an Angelo but she never knew a Lynn. Lynn went up to her mother and told her, "Aalis na ako, ma," went up the street to the main road with a trolleybag full of clothes and her diploma, her transcripts, her bio-data in a plastic envelope under her armpit.

That Sunday, at St. Bernadette's, Lynn found herself on her knees, praying to her Lolo Angel. The first time she felt this desperate was years ago, in a motel in Tagum City. Tiboy, the first man in her life, lay slumped face down on the sheets, part of his dark body covering hers, her right arm free for a cigarette. She was sure she was pregnant and it would be the best time for Lola Glo to appear. It would be her punishment for being so careless, so restless. Not only had Lynn stolen Tiboy away from his farm duties, but she had given him her virginity and officially started her smoking habit.

But the baby never came. She wept with joy at the sight of her lucky blood. Weeks later, she would commit another sin, by leaving him without telling him—"'ni ha, 'ni ho," as they used to say.

Through the years they were apart, Lynn had known— through friends at the bible study group, through the internet—that her town hardly prospered in the years that followed. Local and national elections produced new barangay captains and congressmen, but nothing, no real roads beyond the cracked and pitted path that existed, no real businesses apart from the sari-sari stores and the vulcanizing shops, nothing ever materialized. The barangay hall and the plaza beside it put on new coats of paint and wore them out before the next election, and Lolo Angel would be campaigning again, having a drink with his kumpares at every corner, or alone, while he was plotting his moves.

She thought about the times she saw Lolo Angel, huddled over his bottle and the AM radio. How she wanted to ask him why he drank so much of what he called his "pampagana." It was one of his jokes, to be sure, to be calling a bottle of gin as a way to help the appetite. If anything, she observed but did not tell him, it only helped his appetite for more gin.

And this too, this addiction to alcohol—school had taught her that it was no hobby or habit but a deadly chemical addiction—would she inherit it? Well, if addiction, the pure form of it, was inheritable, then she certainly had it. No sooner than her Marlboro Light was out than she lit another, and with one hand. There was smoothness and girlishness and when she did it that way Tiboy said it was as mesmerizing as watching the pistons of an engine pumping gasoline in delayed synchrony. It had turned into a sort of dance, with a beauty that detached itself from the ugly truth her teachers told her about cancer.

Her grandfather once apologized to her for his drinking. Sins like this were handed down from generation to generation. He didn't know his father or his grandfather, he said, but for his part, he had committed many other bad things and he knew these things were passed on. As she looked at his dull, sad eyes and the white roots of his dyed hair, and she feared the future in store for her. You can't escape it, she thought to herself, that is heredity.

There were pills she could take, exercises she could perform. The other day she had asked a friend about it, speculatively, in a "what-if" tone, who referred her to another friend who had done it. Lynn thought of heading for Lucky Plaza where the rest of her group hung out on Sunday

106

afternoons. Pinays sold that stuff along with thong panties and phonecards. Some of them, she had heard, deposited them in the CRs at Lucky Plaza. One of the papers ran a picture. That was cruel, the decision delayed until five or six months— there was the form already and a little crumpled expression, like the baby was surly because it was too sleepy to wake up.

On a wide avenue clouded by the shade of acacia trees, choked end to end with shopping malls and hotels, she imagined how it would feel. For a moment she thought she could compare the pain of delivering to something she knew. Men wondered, too, she knew, as Tiboy had wondered once. It was a "women only" pain, she explained, like dysmenorrhea. We can't imagine how circumcision feels, she had told him, reaching over for his manhood. Or what it's for, she had added, tracing its odd manmade shape.

But she couldn't imagine childbirth either, she thought, as she stood in the elevator. Gravity bore down as she went up and she grew conscious of her added weight: two cells that weighed like twenty pounds of flesh. She was born six point seven pounds, she remembered. As though birthweight was an important thing: people always feigned a pleasured shock whenever someone was eight-point-something.

And there it was again, lifted by one of those rare Singapore breezes, an invisible thing carried by another invisible thing. Here, she could smell almost nothing, just a faint trace hanging in the air hours after the fruit was split open, but what a trace. Back home, airports and hotels banned it at the height of its season, but they couldn't stop you for bringing it in. After all, there would only be the smell, they couldn't arrest you for it, but it was a fruit you couldn't hide.

She had changed, she felt, perhaps irrevocably, into something she hardly recognized. To her her hands had become rusty, crumpled things, and her feet, bare and swollen rags. Perhaps her child couldn't escape that, too. It would be born limp and tired, overloaded with things it couldn't help but remember. And would it be good to bring something like that into the world? No, it would not be Singapore, but Tagum, or even the town of Mabini. She'd be home, more citified than Tiboy ever really was. Now it was a clump of cells, as one of her friends, before her procedure, explained to her— no, not even—for Lynn, this early on, it would just be a couple of cells, twins cut from the same egg. She had listened and learned enough from high school biology and NatSci in freshman college. A single egg, pierced, split into two, then a geometric progression, then, as Mrs. Gentolia, her high school biology teacher, announced, from years before, "the miracle of life!" Still, an egg, or two half-eggs could not think. They weren't even brain cells. And even if they were, they'd simply be passing that spark of a thought back and forth. It took a million, maybe even a billion, brain cells to formulate the idea of pain, or laugh at a joke, or remember or calculate anything.

108

She was losing time. She needed to think faster than geometric progressions could progress.

Lynn returned very briefly, six years after leaving, for the very first time, from a very separate life and very separate concerns, but gathered and straightened by the sad news of Lolo Angel's death and by the same cracked, pitted dirt road that led from the city. She recognized it: that small-town feeling her friends had told her about. It grew huge inside her as her taxi sped into her town, large and nauseatingly humid, with its dirty sidestreets radiating from the plaza like branches, like thorns.

She remembered the mirror and the long quiet nights and it was time to cry for Lolo Angel, at last. There was their mother, broken at last by something, and it had to be her father's death. No other tragedy had shaken her as much, not the demise of her mother, or of her husband, not even by her departure, eighteen at the time, for college, for Tagum City, and the city after that, and the city after that, and for a good long time.

When she saw her mother she could not help but cry, for her mother and her town, who both were wordless and quiet after all the excitement of her arrival. Her mother ran from inside the house just as Lynn emerged from the tricycle on the dirt path, self-consciously squinting from the heat—more humid, she imagined—since a long time, and they shrieked and their hair stood on end, and embraced and jumped up and down, and finally stood stunned and still, the town and Lynn and her mother, each looking exactly the same as before.

Lynn was the star of the funeral. They made it look like a full reunion. Lynn brought playing card, T-shirts, toiletries, a walkman, a mini-compo and a TV set. There was more and more—new table utensils and drapes from Ikea, costume jewelry, bras and panties— collected over months, gradually deposited into the balikbayan box by her bed. But the biggest surprise was that she had managed to stay—in her mother's embarrassing words, "slim and seductive" as she was six, seven years before when everybody had seen her last. Lynn wanted to say it was all that walking, and you should see the Hong Kong Pinays, but ended up saying "it's the genes, look at you," and they looked at her, pushing sixty, with the loneliest saddest face they had ever seen.

Tiboy sent her a tape. It came in the mail, sent many weeks earlier. The package was there when she got home. It wouldn't fit in the mailslot so they laid it on the mat. She had thought once that he would take her back, Tiboy with his large, enveloping darkness, swallowing her into him. He now lived at the long-winded address on the envelope, an apartment, a street, a subdivision, a district, Tagum City.

She fired up the stereo system. It was automatic to her: first the black box that was the line conditioner, then the amplifiers, then the pre-amplifier, then the CD player and the cassette deck. She waited for the little lights to switch from red to green, pushed the "eject" button, then slid the tape in.

The glowing vacuum tubes on the amplifier threw an almost unbearable heat on her face as she watched the little toothed wheel turning. Lynn heard Tiboy's breathing first, so close to the mic that she flinched. The horrifying sound of his breathing filled the apartment. When his voice came on it sounded funny and tinny, not as she remembered it, beginning with "Angela Lynn...", the pause following it heavy and unsure. Lynn's hands flew swiftly to switch off the tape.

When she curled up to sleep that night she shifted her feverish prayers and wished her patron saint would shift her baby to the Samsons. Kuya Noel would be ecstatic, and Ate Lara would be complete. There would be bridal showers and advance gifts in pink and blue. There was a store in Great World City that was full of things for newborns and their mothers and she had even passed it once, months before. It would be one of those "miracles" Mrs. Gentolia spoke about— something nobody would know about but would set everything truly, instantly right.

The baby would be born and she would be assigned to look after it when they were away. And in those private moments, what would she do with it? She would teach it the same language—they were the same folk after all. She would tell stories. About where she'd been—everywhere: the beach, the mountains, the city. A dozen different houses, done up in a dozen different styles: Victorian, colonial American, Asian fusion and Filipino style. And from all the fast friends she made, she knew much, much more. A lot of it was gossip and stuff about politics back home but there was much more she knew. It wasn't all work, she had learned that from Lolo Angel—it was "official use also."

IN THE HOSPITAL WAITING AREA THERE WAS A WOMAN SITTING BESIDE her, also a Filipina, she could tell, from the shape and weight of her face. The hospital was like a TV hospital, busy and alive and full of equipment, the air smelling of disinfectant and that faint odor of people. She wondered if the silent miracle had occurred and the doctor would give her the usual cold smile instead of writing up an appointment for her at the Ministry of Manpower.

Lynn afforded a thin smile at the woman, with her eyebrows slightly raised in a kind of open gesture. It was not because she merely wanted to be polite, but because she knew Pinoys were prone to making open-ended gestures like that. Here it was a mark of identification that, once returned, rendered strangers instant friends, instant sisters. She made a mental note to make sure that when her amos arrived, nothing would be out of place, and everything, even she, would look untouched. •

Leather

INSTEAD OF TAKING HER USUAL CONNECTING FLIGHT TO ATHENS, Cora decides, on a whim, and also because she is tired of talking to her compatriots and hearing them talk about their jobs, to take the flight twelve hours later. Against her better judgement, she lines up at immigrations, presents her passport and her visa, and drops the name and number of an acquaintance who is housewife to a Frenchman. She follows a crowd of tourists out of the airport and boards the free commuter bus that will take them to the city.

Cora alights at the Avenue Champs-Elysee. The air is brisk, the sky large and low. The buildings are a dirty gray, running into each other in uninterrupted rows. She looks at the Arc, squatting like a tall, overdecorated cake at the end of the boulevard where the roads converge. She scans the near horizon and identifies the tower on her right, its height groping through the clouds. She imagines its size, and how it would look up close.

The avenue is overrun with people getting off cars and buses, browsing and talking shoulder to shoulder at the newspaper stands, clogging the benches and loitering along the storefronts. She has never seen so many well-dressed men and women, in sunglasses and light coats, in suits and boots.

She tightens her step and straightens her clothes. She is wearing her airplane outfit—an old jacket, grey and threadbare, over a light sweater, loose jeans, running shoes. She turns glimpses herself in the storefronts and gallery windows, walking up the avenue, instantly different from the Parisian crowd. She adjusts her sight and sees, in a large boutique window, spring clothes, bright scarves, shoulder bags in brightly colored leather.

She herself has three handbags of the same brand, fakes smuggled out of Shenzhen by a fellow nurse who promised her they were triple-A replicas, exact down to the lining and the zippers. The instant tears in her sisters' eyes were well worth the two weeks' wages total. Now she thinks about them, the black one for Ivy, the brown one for Lisa, and the mustard-colored one she couldn't bear to keep for herself, real leather as far as she could tell, from the sweet chocolate smell to the way the material rippled and wrinkled, to the designer's monogram, two linked letters repeated across the face like speckles on a butterfly's wings.

"If you can help me, please?" The words come from a small Japanese-looking woman, calling to her from around the corner. She is dressed in a cream-colored leather jacket over a white blouse, a mid-length black leather skirt and high boots of the same pale cream. The woman holds up a magazine to her as she speaks. Cora stiffens, holds her handbag tightly against her, thinking about her passport and her cash and her travel documents inside, bound together by a flimsy rubber band that she never changed all these years. Cora thinks she is speaking Japanese—and she has probably mistaken Cora for a Japanese girl, too. This sort of thing has happened before.

At work she has been mistaken for Japanese, or Chinese, or Indonesian, perhaps because of her height, or her slightly slanted eyes, or the undecipherable language she spoke with the other staff. Cora realizes, after careful listening, that the woman is speaking in rudimentary English, sparse and rough. Yes, Cora nods, she understands.

Everything in the Japanese magazine is devoted to one designer brand. There are photos of bags large and small, scarves, sunglasses, umbrellas, keychains, shoes. The woman points out a photograph of a small bag clad in white leather, covered in candy-colored monograms. It has a short strap and a flap secured by a small metal lock. The woman explains that she has already purchased all the colors of the item, including this one: the *Grand Petit multicolore*, by far the rarest of all the sizes and colors, not even on display, and strictly one per customer. That is the problem, she confesses. She has come to Paris only to shop, to buy the *Grand Petit*. That she would be going home with only one *multicolore* would be a shame, a tragedy. Cora returns the woman's plaintive smile with a look of understanding.

With a gloved hand, the woman patiently and carefully indicates the details she must look out for: the small, curved body, the raised, multicolored monograms against the field of white calfskin, the trim in brown suede, the tiny padlock in palladium metal. Cora studies the photo and memorizes the control number.

The plan is simple enough, for Cora to enter the store, calmly request for the bag in question, make the purchase and leave. The woman opens her coffee-colored clutch, takes out a purse and extracts a thick pile of money, from which she counts three thousand Euros into Cora's hand.

114

The contract is sealed with a smile. Cora folds the pale red bills in her hand and stuffs it into the sudden warmth of her pocket. The woman looks at her curiously and Cora agrees—more discreetness is a must. She retrieves the bills, unfolds them, takes out her purse and pushes them inside.

Cora pushes the revolving door and walks into the store, where she is greeted by light music and the faint smell of flowers. She realizes it is the first time she has entered a boutique of this kind. A chandelier dominates the thickly plastered ceiling. Shelves of dark wood lined the walls, and on them the merchandise seem to float and shimmer. A tall door clerk regards the way she looks and greets her with a careful smile and a neutral tone.

Cora briefly tightens her hands into fists to stop them from trembling. She proceeds, quick and purposeful, to the first counter, where a row of scarves is spread out under the glass like a violently colored fan. A tall blond woman behind the counter hesitates for a moment, then welcomes her in French and English. Cora smiles and chooses with a pointed finger. The blond girl pulls the case open, retrieves the scarf, grasps two corners and spreads it out over the counter, the ripples advancing until the field of colors covers Cora's sight and laps at her breast. She fingers the silk, traces the edges of the violets and blues that throw filtered light on her pale brown sweater. "Non," she says, politely, one of the few French words she knows.

A selection of watches runs the length of the next counter, in variations of stainless steel, gold, platinum, simply rendered or adorned with jewels. Cora points out a small one marked with roman numerals and framed by a square bezel in yellow gold. The young woman takes out a small square tray, padded with black velvet. She reaches under the counter, retrieves the watch, and places it with smooth white hands on the tray, turning it so that its face is pointed at her. Cora bends and squints to examine its face, the flattest, shiniest thing she's ever seen. The woman lifts the watch with two hands, unfastens the clasps, and holds it out for her to receive it.

Cora pulls up a jacket sleeve and drapes the watch against her wrist. It is heavier than it looks. She holds out her arm and pulls her head back to regard it from a distance. She brings her wrist close to her face and sees the second hand moving across the numbers with a supernatural slowness and smoothness. Despite herself she holds it up to an ear. Sure enough, under layers of metal silence there is the tight ticking of tiny machinery. From the corner of her eye she sees the tall blonde staring at her.

"A little too small," Cora says. The woman smiles, begins to utter a protest, in halting English, but Cora's attention wanders, past this counter to a column of black shelves, holding rows of shoes, set flush into the stone wall. She lifts a tall-heeled evening shoe from its pedestal, a pump in black patent leather. She runs a finger along almost invisible seams, plays with the straps and buckles and measures the length of its heel against an outstretched hand.

Cora looks at the woman and gives her her size. She sits down on a leather couch, almost collapsing out of exhaustion from the brisk walk up the Champs-Elysee, the long bus ride before that, the queue at immigrations, before that the cramped flight over 18 hours from Manila direct to Paris. She places her bag beside her, removes her running shoes and slips off her white socks, caressing the soles of her feet with a flat, warm palm. The blond girl appears silently, places the shoes tenderly on the marble.floor, and silently helps Cora slip them on her feet.

Before the woman can fasten the straps Cora stands, the high heels making her suddenly shaky and dizzy. She looks down at her feet, in black patent pumps, straps unfastened and free, her pale brown instep exposed from her ankles down to the line where her toes just begin.

She walks back and forth before a gilt-edged mirror laid against the floor, and listens with pleasure to the clicking of her heels, the sound marking her wide, slow gait across the length of the room, softening and slowing as she stops at one shelf, with its silk shirts and blouses, quickening as she moves to the next, laden with purses and wallets. Cora points to a purse, in black, a color she immediately regrets. Her mother forbade her to wear black when she was small because it was too adult, too morbid, too trying hard. And besides what was wrong with wearing pink or bright green like the other girls her age wore? You are always too ambitious, too big-time, you'll wear your health out working too hard!

Cora purses her lips and makes a tiny sigh. She looks at the woman across the counter, who flashes her a brief, impatient smile. The piece is good, but the color is simply too crude, too obvious. Her friends will see her and immediately think it is a fake instead of a true original, bought in the shop on the Champs-Elysee, identifiable only by true collectors, as she remembers from the close-up photos in that woman's catalog, by all the serial numbers in the right place and the clasps in their genuine metal and the right color, by its very shape and weight, the way it lay, plump and smooth and stiff, in the palm of her hand.

"Perhaps Madame would like something bigger, like a bag, non?" the woman says quietly, squinting at Cora's handbag, squeezed under an armpit. She indicates the display case behind her. She takes her through the individual lines, briefly caressing their leather as she names them: the pochette, the French purse, the musette, the saddle bag, the bucket tote, in black, in shades of brown, in white, in three kinds of blue, in leather blindingly smooth, or marked with raised, striped patterns, or printed with squares, symbols or flowers, or the leather etched or printed with monograms, matched with suede, or fabric, or canvas, embellished by gold or silver clasps, or tiny zippers, or simply bound by straps or thongs slipped tightly into hoops.

The door opens. The sounds of the street begin to fill the store and are cut off as the door revolves shut. A soft, plump Frenchwoman walks in, dressed in light furs and smelling of thick perfume. Cora's salesclerk stops, briskly walks out to greet her, smiling widely and speaking sweetly in French. The woman opens her handbag, takes out a pen, scribbles something on a slip of paper and surrenders it to the blond girl. The exchange is brisk, spirited; it ends with flying kisses and a trail of perfume and the swinging door restoring the room to a silence.

"Le *Grand Petit multicolore*," Cora pronounces, carefully and firmly. "S'il vous plait."

This draws a sigh from the blond woman. Another salesclerk, a long-limbed black woman with large, liquid eyes, dressed in the same short blue uniform, turns her head toward her.

"Le *Grand Petit*," the woman repeats, quietly, acquiring a tone of resigned pleasure. She whispers something to the tall black girl, who whispers something back. The blond woman smiles, shakes her head and tells Cora they refrain from letting customers handle items not on display. She takes out the Euro bills and counts them out on the counter, one by one. "Oui.

Le *Grand Petit*," she says, slapping the last bill down, making her decision final.

The black girl disappears briefly into another room and returns with a large box. She places it quietly on the counter, turns it around so that the monogram, two linked letters in stamped gold, faces Cora. The lid is lifted, the layers of white tissue unfurled, and the *Grand Petit* is lifted out into the warm and tender light.

Cora steps out of the pumps and stands on the marble floor in her bare feet. The blond woman kneels before her, carrying her rubber shoes. Cora lets out a tickled laugh as the woman grasps her feet gently and slips them in one at a time.

As Cora exits the store she draws her jacket closer around her. The weak autumn sun temporarily blinds her, and in that moment of blindness she imagines the small Japanese woman is not there anymore, that she has grown tired of waiting for her or forgotten about the matter.

But the little woman is there, right in front of her tracks. Cora adjusts her vision and sees the woman staring wide-eyed at her paper bag. Their toes are almost touching on the sidewalk. Is she afraid that Cora might make a run for it? Cora cannot resist thinking that the woman is suspicious of her. At the same time Cora has begun to entertain the first tendrils of this thought: what if I make a run for it? She sees that the woman has short legs. It will be difficult to run in those boots.

Cora surrenders the shopping bag to her with a smile, remembering how the lock was softly sprung, how the suede flap was easily swept back, how the white leather split open as though it were held together only by liquid tension, like a lip separating from its other, to release a warm vanilla breath. In it she smelled other tones: burnt coffee, the sourness of skin, a trace of sweat. She traced the edge of the inner sleeves, inserting a finger boldly, deepening the crevices, stretching them open, forward and backward, their inner surfaces moist and translucent with softness.

Cora remembers the moment it was returned to its box, the many-hued monograms gleaming on the eggshell-colored leather. She remembers how, years ago, she ended up giving her mustard colored handbag to her mother, who had frowned at it at first. There were other things to spend on—the house needed repairing, the pickup was broken again, and her sisters wouldn't be graduating until the next year. "Don't worry, it's fake," she finally conceded.

Cora hands over the small envelope that holds the authenticity card and the warranty slip. The Japanese woman inspects the contents of the envelope and peeks into the bag. Cora fishes out the fifty-Euro change.

"No. Please, for all your trouble, madame," the woman says, holding out a gloved hand. More smiles are exchanged, and the contract is formally over. The Japanese woman walks down the avenue, toward the Arc, and disappears into the autumn crowd.

Cora opens her handbag, retrieves the fifty Euro bill and slips it into her jeans pocket. She fishes a cigarette out and lights it. She thinks about having dinner at a good restaurant, and perhaps, coffee at a streetside café, if there is still time. •

"Untitled"

SUZETTE, AS SHE INTRODUCES HERSELF, IS IN A THIN YELLOW BLOUSE and a skirt that ends at mid-thigh. She has the easy, unbuttoned style of a company executive after hours.

A half-hour later, we find ourselves in a bar near her place. There's no band, only a DJ standing in a booth in one corner, playing dance music.

Her husband comes home on weekends from his cattle farm in Batangas. She's trying for a baby.

In the foyer of her townhouse a row of cowboy hats, stiff and stained in patches, hangs on the wall. On the tiled floor there are five or six pairs of big cowboy boots, standing straight up, heels and soles caked with dirt, their sharp toes pointed straight at me. She deposits her keys on a small table, where a clutch of pictures is arranged in a tight semicircle. I can make out startling crescents of smiles, the silhouettes of heads and half-bodies against snowy landscapes, white beaches and warmly-lit living rooms.

I follow Suzette up the stairs and into her bedroom's yellow light. I wake with the sky dangerously bluish and the forbidding smell of morning in the air. I fight the urge to return to sleep, but dawn also brings the smell of sex, the warmth of light and the sound of jazz. Eyes still closed, I play games with the upright bass, the kick drum and the snare, the piano and the muted trumpet, its melody delivered so clearly that I can imagine Miles Davis, the cup fixed to his mouth, live and oblivious, turning each labored breath into music. I fix the chords in my ears as they are played: a minor, an augmented, another augmented, a sustained, and then a ninth, the last chord let ring, riding on a single note from his trumpet, a note that holds, within it, other notes, other music.

Suzette moves slightly in the pause between songs. I force my eyes open and see hers tremble under closed lids. Her eyelids open briefly to scan the light outside the window, and close again. She starts humming the dance melody from the bar of the night before.

"They call it trance music," I say into her hair.

"It isn't as bad as the Eurodisco they play in beauty salons," she says. "Or eighties music."

"I kind of like eighties music."

"I love eighties music," she says, smiling. "I was joking."

"I had a band in the eighties. You should've seen us then."

I tell her of how my dad bought me a folk guitar when I was in high school and I learned to play it by looking at the chord charts in music magazines. How I formed a band with friends who did nothing but listen to music all the time and who knew some guitar or had some rhythm. How I found a friend who had some guitar schooling, who knew more licks so he played lead and I played rhythm and sang. The story is a multiplatinum hit.

A band's name is like a ship's name, a horse's name. It needs to be seaworthy and trustworthy. It needs to be lucky. We called ourselves The Jones and Smiths. We were listening to a lot of The Smiths then and loved Junjun Jones. We took names from wordplay, or formed them from inside jokes, or picked phrases out of a book. Nine or ten names in all, for five or six bands, across twenty years, with scores of different guys.

"I remember him," she murmurs. "Junjun Jones. I saw him on the road once, in front of the 70's Bistro. It was four in the morning. He was carrying his guitar case, waiting for a cab. He looked so old and so sad, still doing the same old rock and roll."

Suzette reaches for the remote. Her skin is white, whiter than white, and she would've stood out then, in the eighties, on any given night, in the campus variety shows and benefit concerts, in the Christmas programs and the New Wave parties. The music stops and there's a series of soft clicks as the stereo changes CDs.

I look around slowly in the lazy light. This is her husband's side. On the bedside table there's a brass lamp, an alarm clock and a pile of books: spy thrillers, handgun catalogs, business manuals.

On Suzette's table the lamp has been kept lit through the night. There is a chair stacked high with more reading material: a Larousse cookbook, a manual on home repairs, a coffeetable book on "Designing Small Gardens" and an illustrated guide to house plants.

She notices me looking. "I'm hopeless, huh? I'm planning a small garden around the house."

"You're pathetic," I say. I imagine her squatting on the grass, turning up the soil, thinking about her life. A radio is playing top 40 songs, one of those songs we play every night, and she tilts her head from time to time to hear the ringing of the phone above the music. One of those phone calls could be one of those friends I saw the night before, asking her if she wants to watch the showbands.

Suzette has closed her eyes again. I slide out from under the sheets and lift myself out of bed. The stereo is playing Steely Dan's "Aja"

I walk the smooth wooden floor lightly and tell her of when I played the rebirth of punk and speed metal ten, fifteen years ago. I had a bottle of Red Horse in one hand and the mic in the other. We had a manager, a sound engineer, a roadie. I'd be waiting in the wings while the band thrashed out the intro. Our manager made sure the stage lit up when I went out. The crowd exploded. There were fistfights and rumbles. They threw chairs at us. They loved us.

The groupies came in early and hung around until after the gig. We'd be too tired but worked up at the same time. There were those who came alone and who always thought you were singing to them when you sang. There was a medical student who hung out at Club Dredd on most school nights. It was a jeepney ride away from the University. Her boyfriend listened to Kenny G and Kool and the Gang. After gigs we spent the nights in motels. Then she stopped going to school and started making me nervous. She threatened to kill herself with a scalpel. I told her to fuck off. She took off with my Stratocaster.

Suzette shifts and sits up in bed, following my movements with her eyes. I look at her, cross my arms and attempt a smile. On the stereo it's jazz again, a song played by an acoustic trio, dangerously edging close to the chaos of free time, free form.

"'Green Dolphin Street.' Bill Evans, Right?"

"No," she says. "Chick Corea."

"Well, he's doing Evans," I say.

She arches her eyebrows. "Whatever."

The song is in the middle of an ostinato. I'm sure I've heard this before. I'm a little confused because I've never heard it so bright, so close, so clear.

Suzette gets out of bed and closes all the curtains, one by one. The curtains are white, but thin enough to blunt our shapes into gauzy shadows to prying eyes. Her hair is all over her face and her breasts have suddenly become her eyes, full and clear, with brown nipples for pupils.

The big black remote control has materialized in her hand. The music fades out, retreating into the corners of the room, where I notice, for the first time, thin speakers covered in honeycomb steel, edged in black lacquer, powered by cables thick as a finger.

125

She slips into the bathroom and I listen to the sound of her pee and remember what's in it: three glasses of red wine, a Margarita and a redbull vodka, maybe more. I hear her flush everything down. She hums to herself but I can't pick up the melody. The door opens, and she is in a striped silk robe, but still naked underneath. I approach her and grasp her hips. Her half open mouth smells of toothpaste. She throws a squinty-eyed look at the clock on her husband's table.

"Good morning," she says. I take it to mean goodbye, and hurry. She walks to her bedside table, opens a drawer and picks up a jar of cold cream.

"What's your day like?" I ask.

"Busy. Oh you mean today? Busy. Lots to do, lots to think about. Worry about is more like it."

"Husband trouble," I offer.

"No, just trouble. My husband doesn't give me much trouble nowadays. He's no trouble at all. Which is how we like it. He spends time on his farm."

"Cow trouble."

"Cattle trouble," she says.

I don't even know if they still ride horses on farms, like real cowboys. I think they mostly ride 4x4s now, brand new and pumped up on fat black tires, but always streaked with the kind of dirt you never find in the city, the clean and pure kind. It's dirt from farm, dirt from the homeland. His name recalls that action film star who rode horses, wielded a bullwhip and used twin revolvers on enemies a hundred yards away.

She presses buttons on the remote. The machine clicks obediently. New music comes on, the stuff they call downbeat, anonymous and sophisticated, the kind they play in cafes and designer boutiques.

Our biggest break was Japan, or almost. Someone was opening a new club and they wanted a Filipino band to play. They held the audition at a KTV joint in Malate. It was deserted. It smelled of shit and there were rats in the seat cushions. Our manager made us rehearse a new repertoire that included pop and slow rock. I felt uneasy learning licks and lyrics from Scorpion and Journey and Toto, but we'd heard the older sessionists talk about life on the road, life with the band, playing clubs on Boat Quay, or in Lan Kwai Fong, or even in the half-empty lobby lounges in Bangkok hotels. I wanted to hear my voice, my sound, spilling out across the world, never mind that I'd be singing Queen's "Bohemian Rhapsody" or Toto's "Africa" night after night to a small crowd that, they said, mostly thinned into a handful of homesick Pinoys. Better that way, they told me, or else I'd be playing all night to some strangers and then I'd be the one sick of loneliness.

We played our hearts out, played all night, but the club manager ended up picking a female vocal trio who wore cocktail dresses and sang Bananarama songs through headset mics. After that we split up for a while, then found a new name, new management, and a new life playing nightclubs, karaoke joints, parks and pizza parlors. By that time The Smiths had split up. The Dawn were gone. Color It Red had changed vocalists and The Youth just disappeared. I made connections with jinglemakers and advertising producers, finding among them old bandmates, old hangers-on, and new opportunities to get by.

By day I sell life insurance and real estate, calling old friends, looking up old acquaintances, recruiting them for my sales network, arranging to meet them at malls or coffee shops. Occasionally I play rhythm guitar for a friend who does karaoke versions of hit songs that are identical note-for-note, or sing for jingles and radio stingers adapted from the first few bars of pop songs.

When I return to the bedroom, the light has brightened and stretched itself out fully.

"Gotta go," I announce. "Got work to do. Lots of people to call."

Downstairs, in the morning light, everything looks fresh and peaceful. There are flowers in a vase. Beside the ashtray is a notepad with quickly written things. I cannot resist looking: the writing is almost illegible and I don't recognize the names or the numbers.

When I had the old band we had a formula: three songs, then a short spiel, another four or five numbers, then another spiel to introduce the last three numbers. Ten songs made a forty-five minute set. Three sets gave us gate receipts for the night, money enough to eat and drink some more and take a cab home, with some left over.

There were times I'd see them connect, swaying and mouthing the words. I'd be untouchable and unreachable. Our music broke into a wail, soaring and diving all at once. On a good night there'd be spontaneous applause. Then I'd strum the opening riffs to the one song I'd written—"Untitled."

By the end of the set there'd be four or five empty bottles on the stage. The last bottle I would shake over the audience's heads. I'd seen Sid Vicious do that in a film they'd made of him. At the end of the film he had gotten so drunk and so stoned that he set fire to himself and his girlfriend while they were in bed.

128

I exit the living room without touching anything, without trying out the keys on the upright piano, without even looking at the pictures of strangers on the table. I hear the music turn louder in the bedroom upstairs.

On my way out I see the cowboy boots and the row of cowboy hats above it. I take the newest-looking hat and put it on my head. The fit is snug and ready. I walk out and the light is strong and bright. I head straight toward the sound of the highway and disappear into the horizon. •

Glossary

White elephants
KTV   Karaoke TV

Procession
Lola   Grandmother
Taglish   Tagalog-English
Monggo   mung
Sukang tuba   coconut sap vinegar
Tiyo   Uncle
Tiya   Auntie
Lechon   roasted suckling pig
Dinuguan   blood stew
Embotido   meatloaf
Tilapia   a species of flatfish (*Tilapia nilotica*)
Pancit   noodles

Thousand year eve
Media Noche   traditional New Year's Eve dinner

Nilda
Bagoong   fermented shrimp paste
"Uban ko nimo" "Let me go with you" (Visayan)

Ghosts
Kuya   Elder Brother
"otso-otso"   dance popularized by a noontime variety show
Ate   Elder Sister
"amoy ewan"   "smelling of I-don't-know-what"
FMD   Foot-and-Mouth Disease
'Mariosep   Short form of "Hesus, Maria, Hosep!"
         or "Jesus, Mary and Joseph!"
"Aalis na ako, Ma." "I'm leaving, 'Ma."
"'ni ha, 'ni ho"   without a word
Pampagana   appetizer

ANGELO R. LACUESTA was born in 1970. His first book, *Life Before X and Other Stories*, won the Madrigal-Gonzalez Best First Book Award and the National Book Award. •